Karma's
Deadly Kiss

Edward C. Knox

Fulton Books
Meadville, PA

Published by Fulton Books 2024

ISBN 979-8-89221-695-1 (paperback)
ISBN 979-8-89221-696-8 (digital)

Printed in the United States of America

Part 1

Hole in the Wall

Kansas City, Missouri, 2006

Somewhere downtown, there was a certain hole-in-the-wall nightclub jumping. Benny's Juke Joint had the Jimmy Tomo's Revue on stage jamming the blues away. Benny Tucket, the club owner, walks in swaying an old leather briefcase, looking rather stern.

Tom Northberg, the manager, walks up to him. "Hey, man, you got my loot?" Benny frowns even harder and replies, "Look, I don't need to be hit with this shit as soon as I walk in!"

Tom shouts back, "Heyyy, I'm just sayin'…I need my money, Ben! It's been two months already. I feel I've been patient enough!"

Now really frustrated, Ben blasts, "Look, I've told you before… I'll shoot you your damn money as soon as I'm able, okay! Stop pestering me and get back to work please!" He immediately storms off as Tom looks on. The music and noise from the crowd blare in the background.

Time passes, and Ben emerges from his office. Surveying the club, he spots the bartender and walks over. "Hey, Rod, have you seen Arleen? She's supposed to be performing."

Rodney Baines, the youthful bartender, replies, "Naw, boss, she hasn't flowed through yet."

Ben smirks, then sarcastically says, "Umm-hmm…and she's about to flow up outta here permanently if she can't get her ass in here on time!"

Suddenly, the club door opens, and the club singer sashays in. The bouncer smiles, then gives her a wink as he steps aside to let Arleen Powers through. Ben stares at her angrily, with his arms crossed, as she approaches. The sarcasm continues as he blurted,

"Well, well, well, comin' in all diva style, huh? At least you decided to show up."

Instantly, she puts up a hand and replies, "Look, Ben, I know I'm late and speakin' of late, you owe me money, nigga! You haven't paid me for the last two performances."

Rod turns away chuckling, holding his hand over his mouth.

Putting up both hands, Ben lashes out, "You better *chill* on that, woman!" then gazes at Rod, "And what the hell you laughin' at!"

Immediately, Rod straightens up and rushes to the other end of the bar to take care of a customer. Standing with her arms crossed and with much attitude, Arleen smacks her lips then says, "Well… what's it gonna be, Ben?"

He replies, "Get yo ass on stage or beat it! Take your pick. I'll give you your cash when I have it!"

She puts one hand on her hip and one finger in his face now about to go off on him when suddenly he winks at the MC on stage. "Okay, ladies and gentlemen, put your hands together for the lovely and talented Arleen Powers!"

The crowd erupts. She rolls her eyes at Ben and mouths the words while pointing at him, "I'm gonna get you," then she turns toward the crowd, smiles, and waves as she makes her way to the stage. As soon as the spotlight finds her, the band begins, and she starts to sing. Scanning the audience, Arleen eventually makes eye contact with Ben, frowns, rolls her eyes, and quickly turns away. With a devilish smile, he turns and walks back to his office.

Later on, after the performance, Tom, Arleen, and Rod are congregated at the bar. They're conversing about their dilemma with Ben.

"He's been puttin' me off for two freakin' months, now. Mannn…I'm tired of it! Hell, I need my money," gripes Tom.

"Pssshh…honey, I feel ya. Hell, the nigga hasn't paid me for the last two—oh no, wait…the last three performances now. Yet…he's gonna talk shit about me being late tonight? Whatever!"

Rod laughs as he replies, "You know I've been noticing how cheap brotha really is."

4

Tom interjects, "No, *cheap*'s not the word. He's just a plain *asshole*!"

Arleen bursts into laughter, then says, "Wow, enough said. Anyway, excuse me, fellas, but a sista's gotta go to the ladies' room."

As she's walking away, Tom replies, "Yep, I need to go take care of some business myself." Soon they both disappear to the back of the club.

Ben's in his office going over some figures while talking to himself, "Damn, these bar receipts are coming up short again. I know one of them bastards is robbin' me. Shit, probably both!" Now the telephone rings. Flustered, he casts aside the paperwork and answers it, "Hello?"

The woman on the other end speaks, "Hey, Ben, you sound kind of frustrated about something. What's up?"

He sighs loudly, then blasts, "What the hell do you want!"

"Hey, you need to calm down, Ben! I was just callin' to see if you've considered my proposal. I'm in the building—"

He interrupts, "Look, bitch...I'm in no mood for this shit tonight! I have enough to deal with and—"

She interrupts, "You good-for-nothing son of a bitch! I oughta come back there and put my foot up—"

He interrupts again, "You ain't gonna do shit but shut the hell up!" then slams down the receiver. Talking to himself again, totally enraged now, "Shit, I can't believe this bitch is still tryin' to buy my place! Nobody's gonna get this joint, nobody!" as he slams his fist down on the desk.

Ranetta Gibbs throws her cell phone into her purse seemingly ticked off. She storms toward the bar, then blurts, "Excuse me... excuse me!" flagging down the bartender. He walks over to her and then she asks, "Where exactly is Mr. Tucket's office?"

"Umm, do you have some business with him because I can go get him. What's your name?"

"Oh, no...never mind. I'll just deal with his ass later. Thanks, anyway."

Rod smirks, nods, and turns his attention back to the other customers. She heads for the restroom in the back.

Ben's still in his office balancing the books when suddenly he shudders! A deep chill streaks down his spine as he whirls around to stare at the blank wall behind him, sensing something. Somehow he knew what was about to happen. He straightens up in his chair and turns back around, then blurts out, "I know you've come for me. I don't know exactly who, but if you do it, trust me, I'll come back and take you and all those that were against me…back to hell with me!"

Then…*bang!* A single gunshot rings out from behind the wall. The bullet rips through and sails right into the back of Ben's skull, knocking him forward to his immediate death. Now slumped over his desk, blood trickles slowly down his neck onto the paperwork below. Benny Tucket is finished, but by whom?

The Investigation

Beyond the flashing lights of the investigators' cameras stand Tom, Arleen, Rod, and Ranetta, shocked but not saddened by the sudden murder of Benny Tucket. All seemingly have a motive to do the evil deed of revenge. Of course, the police have no clue of the motive; nevertheless, they're all suspects for now.

Time passes, and none of the suspects could be held accountable for the murder. Marco Edison, the club DJ, told one of the detectives in an interview, "The only person I knew Ben had beef with was a dude named Theo Haze."

Theo was a neighborhood thug and part-time pimp. He would pop up from time to time at the club. Marco recalled a time when Theo and Ben got into an altercation in the club. Later, when things simmered down, he went to ask Ben what all the drama was about and if he needed Big G to get involved. Big G was the bouncer, Glenn Johnson. He said that Ben told him that it wasn't necessary and that he could handle the two-bit bitch-ass himself. Marco also added that he asked Ben, "Why the beef?"

He said, "To make a long story short, he took my baby away from me a while back."

Confused, Marco said he asked, "Baby? What baby? You had a child?"

He was like, "No, man, not a little child...my daughter. That bastard took away my baby. She started dating him, and shortly after that, they disappeared."

Two days later, the authorities locate Theo and bring him in for questioning. The interrogation begins. "So let's have it, Mr. Haze. Where were you a couple of days ago?"

"I told you...I ain't dealin' dope or pimpin' no more."

The detective blasts, "That's not what I asked you. Just answer the question!"

"Okay, okay. Damn! I was at my baby mama's house. I'll admit, I smoked a li'l weed…"

The other detective that was in the room interrupts, "Yeah, we already know that much," then drops a folder full of documents, which spread out across the table in front of Theo. He jabs his finger down on top of the folder and yells, "Your mile-long rap sheet suggests all of that! What we wanna know is…what beef did you have with Benny Tucket that would motivate you to put one in his head?"

Totally thrown by this accusation, he blurts, "What the fuck, dude! I wasn't even nowhere in the area of the club that night! You know what, I'm not sayin' another word without a lawyer present, not another word!"

One of the detectives sighs loudly and turns away while the other gathers up all the documents back into the folder. "Fine, Mr. Haze, you're free to go, but I wouldn't leave town anytime soon."

Theo stands as he remarks, "Whatever…we'll see what my lawyer has to say," then storms out of the room.

Days later, as the investigation continues, Theo's alibi checks out. A week passes, and no longer a suspect, he dips out of town. A couple of months go by, and the case eventually goes cold.

A New Year

It's 2007, and a certain hole-in-the-wall nightclub is still jumping! It's simply called the Wall now, and Arleen Powers is on stage rockin' the crowd with her blend of R & B and jazz flavor. Backing her up is the Jimmy Tomo's Revue, still the band of choice.

Ranetta Gibbs, the new owner, walks in and greets Tom with a smile. The manager extends a hand to her and says, "Hey, Netta, the place is jumpin' tonight. It hasn't been like this for a while."

She shakes his hand and explains, "Well, Tom, we make a great team. We've managed to keep it all together after the tragedy."

Smiling, he scopes the place and replies, "Yep, I think you're right about that."

She says, "Well, if you'll excuse me, I have to go back and finish cleaning out the old office so I can put up those storage shelves I bought yesterday."

"Do you need my help?"

"No, I can manage. Besides, you need to keep an eye on the place." She gives him a wink. He nods, then she turns and disappears to the back.

In Ben's old office, Ranetta's sweeping the floor when she notices the bullet hole in the wall. Pausing for a moment, she reminisces about the previous events. She shakes it off and continues sweeping. All of a sudden, the broom strikes a loose piece of tile that was slightly sticking up from the floor. It slides across the room. Looking down, she spots something that was underneath the tile. It was a journal of some kind. She reaches down to pick it up and discovers there were two more beneath it. Gathering them up, she simply puts them in one of the large storage bins that were scattered about the room. Ranetta feels a certain creepiness come over her now. She whirls around to see Arleen standing there, smiling.

"Ohhh, lawd! Child, you scared me! Why the hell you creepin' up on folks like that?"

Sarcastically, she replies, "I'm not creepin' around. I just simply walked in so...anyway, is this gonna be your new office?"

"No, actually me and Tom will be sharing his office. I'm gonna utilize this space for storage. Why? What's up?"

"Oh, nothing much. I just figured since that shiftless bastard Ben never gave me the money he owed, this area could be converted into a dressing room for me."

"Now hold on...I know he did you and a lot of other people wrong, but unfortunately, there's nothing that can be done about that now."

Arleen quips, "So in other words, the answer's no!"

Shrugging, she answers, "Well, hey—"

Arleen interrupts, "You know what...there is something you can do, Netta. There's been rumors floatin' around about Ben hidin' money in this joint over the years. If you somehow come across it, you could break a sista off a li'l something, something. You ain't gotta go tell nobody nothing. Feel me?"

Ranetta immediately puts a hand up and says, "First of all, I've never heard of any rumors like that. Besides, he was broke! I doubt if he had any to stash."

Arleen insists, "I'm just sayin'...don't forget about me, alright?"

"Alright, whatever!" Arleen nods, turns, and walks out the room as Ranetta looks on in frustration, confused about this chick's attitude all of a sudden. Once again, chills run up and down her spine. She turns to stare at the bullet hole in the wall. There's a strange presence lurking beyond it—she feels it! She walks to the door and looks out—nothing! *What is it?* was the question burning in her mind.

Later, Ranetta steps into her office to find Tom intensely searching for something all over the place. She can tell that he's already looked behind the file cabinets because they were all twisted and away from the wall. Now he's moving his desk out of the way when she asks, "Excuse me...what are you doing, Tom?"

Startled, he drops the desk and whirls around, "Oh, damn! You scared me half to death!"

Startled herself, she jumps and says, "Damn...sorry! What are you looking for—money?"

With a silly look on his face, he hesitates before answering, "No...why would you ask me something like that?"

"Well...Arleen just hit me with this silly notion earlier this evening that Ben was hidin' money around here. Do you know anything about that?"

He shrugs, and with a nervous laugh, he answers, "Well... umm...I was lookin' for that order form for the new equipment we're supposed to be getting."

Confused, she asks, "Huh, equipment? What equipment?"

Tom stands there looking around as he answers, "Yeah, you remember? The equipment for the DJ booth."

Then it dawns on her, "Oh yeah!"

He peers behind the desk, "I know I left it in here somewhere. I filled it out and everything."

Though skeptical but not showing it, she says, "Don't worry about that this minute. We'll deal with it later. You need to go out and check on the club. I'll finish cleaning up, then prepare to lock it down shortly, okay?"

Halfway paying attention and still looking around, he replies, "Okay...I'll go talk to Marco."

"Good, you do that." Looking on as he leaves the office, she shakes her head.

She moves the desk back into place and couldn't help but notice in one of the trays on the desk was an unfilled order form for Ellis Electronics. Bewildered, she picks it up and gazes at it for a moment, then places it back in the tray. Shaking her head again as she's walking toward the light switch, Ranetta pauses at the doorway, looks around, and notices the file cabinets are still in disarray. She shrugs, waves her hand, then turns off the light and closes the door, then locks it. In the dark hallway now, she feels those same chills creep up, causing her to hurry into the main area of the club. Tom's over chatting with the bartender. The noise in the place has died down tremendously. The DJ is starting to pack up for the night. As she walks past Tom, she says, "Be careful locking up, Tom. I'll see you tomorrow."

"I will…you take care," then continues his conversation with Rod. She waves at Marco while making her way toward the entrance. He nods at her as she passes. The bouncer greets her at the door. "Hey, Netta, I can walk you to your car."

Immediately, she says, "Whoa…thank you! Especially tonight, Glenn…I've been havin' some funny feelings since I got here."

With a concerned look on his face, he asks, "Really? What kind of feelings?" Walking outside now, they head for her car as she replies, "I can't exactly explain it, but they're strange feelings…you know, like something's gonna happen."

Pausing for a moment before answering, "Hmm…it might be a simple case of woman's intuition."

She laughs and blurts, "Okay…but what? I'm sure you got somethin' there, Big G, but I don't have a damn clue what it is. Oh, well…I'm not gonna worry about it anymore." Unlocking her door, she gets in and says, "Thank you for walking me to my car and listening to me rant."

Glenn laughs and says, "Oh…it's no problem at all. You have a good night and please be safe."

"Oh…I will. See you tomorrow night, okay?" Then he closes her door. She starts the engine, waves, and pulls out of the parking lot as he looks on.

The following evening, it's the same routine. Arleen's on stage doing her thing with the band. There's a bit more of a crowd, as the bartender and waitresses are busy serving up drinks to the customers. Ranetta enters and surveys the place, eventually spotting Tom by the DJ booth chatting with some partygoers. He happens to look in her direction and waves. She waves back, then continues on to their office. She opens the door, walks in, and stops short. Totally stunned, she's greeted by an office completely rearranged! All the new shelves are up, reference books and folders placed neatly and in order on them. The new computer is up and running.

Wow! she thinks. *What brought this on, I wonder?*

Meanwhile, Arleen finishes up her set as the crowd cheers and applauds. The MC takes the stage and thanks the crowd, then makes a few announcements as she leaves the stage. Tom walks up from behind and grabs her arm as he slightly tugs her close. He bends down and whispers in her ear, "I need to talk to you for a second."

They stroll over to the bar when she turns and asks, "So...what's up, Tom? What's on your mind?"

He frowns and chuckles as he says, "So where the hell did you get that crazy notion that Ben's got some money stashed away around here?"

She puts a hand on her hip, smacks her lips in frustration, and exclaims, "See, first of all, I told that heifer not to say anything to anybody! Secondly...what's it to you, anyway?"

Tom raises a hand and replies, "Whoa...remember that asshole owed me money, too. I've searched his old office as well as mine—nothing! Nada! Didn't find a damn thing. So...that's why I'm asking you—what have you heard?"

Arleen hesitates for a second before answering, "I've just heard that the ole' tight-ass used to hide it away, frontin' like he was always broke." He folds his arms as he puts a fist under his chin and says, "You know what...I just thought about something. Ben was tight with that crazy-ass dude down the street, you know...the one that ran the novelty shop."

Scrunching up her face, she blurts, "What the hell does Voodoo Child got to do with this?"

"Well, hell...I mean, him and Ben seemed to be close or something. He would always go over there to talk to him. I remember asking him once if they were related. His response was no, that they were just good friends and that they went way back."

Still confused, Arleen asks, "Ohh-kay...once again, what does Voodoo Child got to do with anything?"

Kind of flustered now, he states, "Look, all I'm sayin' is that maybe he hid the money somewhere over there. You know he owned that building, too." Her eyes widen, shocked by what he just said. "What...are you serious? I didn't know that at all!"

"Yeah...not to mention Voodoo Child disappeared right after Ben was murdered." Now with a slight pause, they look at one another, pondering on what he just said.

Tom speaks up first, "Damn...I wonder if Voodoo Child had something to do with it?"

She shrugs and says, "I didn't even know him. I've just heard about him from various sources who had actual contact with him. You know what, Tom...he could've found that money, popped Ben, and skipped town."

He shakes his head in agreement and replies, "Wow...I don't know, Arleen, you could be right, but seriously, I would like to investigate it further just to be sure!"

Confused again, she asks, "Investigate what? What do you mean?"

He starts to explain, "First off, the shop was left abandoned, and it hasn't been knocked down yet. I figure...he had to have a safe over there, too. You know...tucked away somewhere...Anyway, the city, I'm sure, has confiscated the property and doesn't know what to do with it yet. That's probably why the building's still standing. All the doorways and windows have been boarded up."

She interrupts him, "Yo...hold on. That's not necessarily true. Someone else could have bought the property."

"Yep...that's true, but who's gonna buy property like that and let it sit there for a whole year and not do anything with it? I'd like to sneak in and find that safe. I've heard nothing has been removed from the premises."

"Tom, come on. How could you know that a safe really exists, and if it does, Voodoo Child could have already hit it. Man...I wouldn't run the risk of getting caught and bein' slapped with a breaking and entering charge, especially for nothing!"

"Hey...I just want to exhaust all possibilities...After all, Arleen, that bastard owes us big time."

"Yeah, yeah...you're so right about that, but it's certainly not worth the risk, though, Tom. Yes, I know you're a grown-ass man, and you're gonna do what you want to do anyway. That's fine...but I'm starting to feel like Netta is right. There's nothing that can really be done now. I'm just gonna leave it alone." He gestures as if to say okay, but then says, "I understand…but now if I do find something, then what?"

She smirks and replies, "Then I guess it's yours unless…you wanna break a sista' off…a li'l something, something," singing that last part like the song by Maxwell.

He laughs at the clever remark and says, "See…that's what I thought! You ain't foolin' nobody, lady!"

She laughs and says, "Anyway…I'm outta here. I'll see you tomorrow."

"Alright, Ms. Powers, I'll holla."

Arleen goes to the back to get her things before she leaves. As she's gathering her belongings, something grabs her attention. Turning toward the wall, she stands there for a moment, looking. Now transfixed on the bullet hole, she decides to approach it and peer through. Nothing's there! Turning back around, she shakes it off and goes to retrieve her bag when…"Psst!" She jumps in complete shock, spins around, and stares in total horror! Arleen's eyes widen as she blurts out, "Wha-wha-what are you doing here? Oh my god!" She backpedals as she screams, then trips and falls flat on her back. She puts up her hands to shield her face. Completely frantic, she screams a bloodcurdling scream that resounded throughout the entire club! Seconds later, the screaming stops.

Tom is the first to make it to the back as he darts from the DJ booth. Ranetta hurries out of the office and almost runs into him at the doorway of the storage room. They stand there in terror, wondering what the hell just happened. Arleen's on her back, seemingly unconscious. Tom runs over to feel for a pulse—there isn't one! He hangs his head in sadness as a crowd gathers at the door, gasping and a few screaming in the background. Ranetta hesitates before asking, "Is she…gone, Tom?"

He looks up, tears were streaming down his face, nods, and in a faint whisper, "Yeah…she's gone."

"Oh my god!" screams Ranetta, then falls to her knees. Those around her come to comfort her as the tears flowed and bore witness to the sudden tragedy before them.

Two weeks later, Arleen Powers is buried on February 8, 2007. The cause of death, surprisingly to all, was a heart attack! Ranetta sits in her office, puzzling over this outrageous fact. *How the hell does a healthy thirty-something-year-old woman suddenly die of a heart attack?* she thinks. *The doctors suspected something extremely traumatic had to happen to trigger it.* Then she asks herself out loud, "But what?"

A familiar voice from behind asks, "But what, what?"

She turns to see Tom in the doorway. He walks in and sits down at his desk. She explains, "I'm totally confused about Arleen's death, Tom. It doesn't make any sense! The doctors basically said that something spooked her so intensely that it triggered a heart attack. Okay... we did hear her scream before we found her dead on the floor, but no one was there! Did you see anyone or anything run from the back or out of the club?"

"No."

"Okay...so what could've caused her so much trauma so fast and so intensely? They didn't find any drugs in her system at all."

Confused himself, Tom replies, "Wow, good question! First of all, I don't know what could've caused all that. Like you, I didn't see anyone come out of that room. Secondly, the back doors were still locked and chained when I checked them shortly after the incident. Both restrooms were checked as well."

Ranetta shakes her head in disgust, then says, "Damn it, Tom... I'm lost! I just don't get it!"

"Yep...I'm lost, too! You're right...It doesn't make sense, and I don't mean to sound like an insensitive jerk when I say this, but... umm...you know we have to find new talent. The band's having a tough time finding a new vocalist."

She nods and answers in a sullen voice, "Yeah...yeah, I know we do."

"Do you have anyone in mind?"

Kind of staring off into the distance, she answers, "Yes...as a matter of fact, there is someone."

A Fresh Face

The Wall now has a few changes, one of them being a new band. The new ensemble, Premier, hosted a different sound and vibe for the club. Jazz with a dash of funk here and there was strictly their thing! The second change was vocalist, Valencia, the new face. She's a lot younger, somewhat more physically appealing, and vocally talented than Arleen was. The band's already on stage moving the crowd with their intoxicating sound. The lights dim slowly as they wrap up their set. Applause erupts as the band suddenly stops and the place goes black. A spotlight flashes on and Calvin, the club MC, appears, then says, "Thank you! Thank you! Give it up for Premier!" The applause grew louder along with a few cheers. "Now I want to bring to the stage for the second night the lovely and talented Valencia!" The cheers and applause continued as Val takes the stage.

Theo Haze enters the building, scoping the place, eventually focusing his attention toward the stage. Standing there for a second, he smirks then finds his way to the bar. He grabs a seat and orders a drink. "Hey...yo, Rod! What's goin' down, playa? Can a brotha get some Patron on ice?"

He looks up and smiles, then laughs as he walks over to give him a high five. "Damn...what's up, dawg? Yo, it's been a minute!"

Theo laughs and says, "Yep, it's been a minute. I just got back in town a few days ago. The place looks good. I'm diggin' the new vibe!"

Rod remarks as he's fixing his drink, "Yeah, it's come a long way since Ben had the joint. Netta's doin' good things, and this singer... whoa...I'm feelin' this new singer, dawg! I mean, I would love to literally! Whoa!" They both laugh as Theo replies, "Well, hell...I can make that happen for ya, playa."

Rod looks with a devilish smirk, then asks, "Word?" He takes a sip of his drink then answers, "Word!" Someone at the other end of the bar's trying to get Rod's attention, so Theo quickly says, "Yo, dude... go handle your business. I'll get back at cha about that later, alright?"

Rod laughs as he walks away, blurting out, "You do that, playa!" Theo turns his attention back to Val as she continues performing. Slowly, he sips on his drink, lost in thought.

Meanwhile, Tom has the night off, so he decides to snoop around the abandoned building down the street. Ignoring the signs marked "Prohibited" posted on the boarded-up doors and windows, he breaks into the building. Lurking about the dark for a second or two, he finally turns on his flashlight. Panning it around, he spots sparingly stocked shelves along the wall. Trash is all over the place, things toppled over as if the building had been ransacked. Cautiously, he makes his way to the back of the store. Flashing the light around the room, he spots an old voodoo shrine. Continuing to pan the flashlight about, he sees various-sized candles on shelves, tables, and on the floor. Suddenly, two rats dart in and out of the beam of light, startling him. "Goddammit!" He drops the flashlight on the floor. He reaches down to retrieve it when...he thinks he hears something. Hesitating while listening in the darkness, a strange feeling comes over him. He turns and flashes the light at the shrine. Instantly there's a clicking sound, then a loud clank, followed by a low creaking sound. It was like someone opening something. All the while, Tom is flashing the light around the shrine, trying to get a glimpse of what was going on. Nothing! Walking closer, he reaches forward to cast aside the wicker material that's hanging from the wall above the shrine. Much to his surprise, there was a safe deep inside the wall, and the door was open! Flashing the light inside, he spots a couple of stacks of money rubber-banded together, a knife, and a gold chain with a gold pendant connected to it, encircled with diamonds. He reaches in and pulls out all the contents, then goes to the middle of the floor to lay everything out. Sitting the flashlight on the floor next to the items, he picks up each stack of money and counts them in the light. He folds one up and places it in his pants pocket, then the other in his jacket pocket. Suddenly, there's a loud clanging noise up front. He grabs the flashlight and takes off to investigate. Flashing the light just in time, he catches a glimpse of cats creeping out of the store through the entrance he busted through. Relieved that that's all it was, he turns and goes back to the room. As he enters, that strange feeling comes back again. Tom now finds the gold chain and picks it up, but...no knife. He shrugs it off, smiling in the darkness because he counted out two grand and figured the chain would definitely be worth something. He lets out a little laugh as he starts to walk out of the room. Then *slam!* Out of nowhere, the door of the room closes. All the candles around the room begin to illuminate one by one! Totally freaked out, Tom screams out, "What the fuck! Who's there? What's goin' on?" He frantically looks in every direction. Then just like that, all the candles blew out! He stands in the dark, panting loudly, then from behind he hears, "Psst!" He whirls the flashlight around. Nothing! Now he rushes for the door and tries to open it. It doesn't budge! He yanks and yanks on the doorknob...nothing! Leaning his head on the door, trying to control his breathing, he asks, "Wha-wha-what do you want? You want your money back? Huh? Is that what you want?" He slowly turns in the darkness. A few heart-pounding seconds go by, then a candle is lit about six inches from his face. He lets out a bloodcurdling scream when he witnesses the image that briefly flashes before his eyes. The knife that was mysteriously missing flies out of nowhere and is sunk deep into his chest. Tom falls to the side with a thud on the cold concrete floor. Flames immediately erupt all around the room, eventually engulfing his body.

Thirty minutes later, Ranetta's headed for the club. She approaches the blockade as the police wave her around the inferno that was consuming the old building. Ranetta stares in shock, wondering what had caused it to go up in flames. Funny feelings grew inside as if she already knew the deal! Shaking it off, she continues on down the road. She pulls into her usual parking space, turns off the engine, and sits for a moment gathering her thoughts. Grabbing her cell phone, she decides to give Tom a call just to check on him. The phone rings at his apartment, and eventually his answering service picks up. She leaves a message. "Hey, Tom...this is Netta. I was just checkin' on you. That old building down the street from the club is burnin' to the ground right this minute! It's nine thirty-eight now. Give me a call as soon as you get this message, okay? Thanks, bye," then she hangs up, gets out of the car, and heads for the club entrance.

Val, who has long since finished her set, is about to leave when Theo stops her. "Well, well, well...I finally catch up to my number one."

"Look, Theo...I ain't got time fo' no games please! Not tonight, okay?"

He puts up a hand and says, "Ain't no games, woman! You know what time it is, remember? You owe me." She rolls her eyes and says, "I don't owe you nothin'!"

"Bitch, please! On the contrary, don't make me have to remind you." She sighs loudly as he continued his assault. "It's time for you to get back in the damn game—ho!"

Val drops her head for a few seconds, then looks him square in the face and says, "Man...I've got this new gig right now! I'm fulfilling a dream, Theo—I'm singin'!"

He laughs and says, "Okay...so who said you had to stop? This shit is a perfect front! What, you got a dressing room or whatever back there? Hell, you can take the tricks back and handle yo' bizness! You know what I mean, Mommy?"

She hesitates for a second before responding. Shaking her head, Val replies, "Damn, Theo...I don't know about all that! I might get caught, or even worse, I'll go back to jail! I'm not having that!"

Shaking his head, he says, "No, you won't...not if you're discreet with it. Trust me, you'll be straight."

Val blurts, "Theo...when am I gonna have time to find tricks? I'm tryin' to go back to school, too!" Now a little more frustrated, he exclaims, "Damn, you doin' too much, woman! Besides, I've got all that taken care of! I've got a few customers in line already, baby. You just need to stay focused, do you hear me? I need my fuckin' money! Unless you want me to take it out yo' ass, bitch! It's your choice."

Flustered, Val walks away with her arms crossed as tears start to flow. Eventually, she vanishes out the front door.

It's Saturday night, and the Wall's jumping as usual except something's missing! In fact, make that *someone's* missing. Ranetta walks up to Rod and taps him on the shoulder when he almost jumps clean out of his skin, completely startling her in the process. "Whoa... damn! Sorry about that Netta. I'm just slightly jumpy tonight! I don't know why, but it's like something very strange has come over me."

She exclaims, "Wow, are you serious? I've been having strange feelings myself."

"Yeah...it's like something bad is gonna happen again." She pauses before asking him, "Hey...have you seen or heard from Tom tonight?"

"Nope...I ain't seen him at all." She exhales deeply, then says, "I have a bad feeling something has happened to him, Rod. He hasn't returned my calls or anything. I've been tryin' to reach him since last night—nothing!"

Calming down a bit, Rod states, "He'll probably show up sooner or later. He might've had a serious emergency, you know...A family member or something and had to leave town unexpectedly."

Ranetta, now a bit calmer, replies, "You might be right, but hell, he still could call and let somebody know something!"

It's a week later. Still no word from Tom, and the Wall has acquired another hole! This time, figuratively. Val has sunk back into the life she so desperately tried to escape. She's in the back taking care of business with a john in the storage room when she senses a presence beyond the bullet hole in the wall. Soon, she dismisses it as maybe a perve getting his kicks. Minutes pass, and the john emerges from the room, smiling crazily while zipping his pants up. He walks out to the main area of the club and is greeted by Ranetta.

"Hey, Rod...whatcha doin' here on your night off? I guess you can't get enough of this place, huh?" With a stupid look on his face, he answers, "Well...I guess you could say that."

Peering beyond him, she notices Val coming from the back, and while eyeing her, she asks, "Why were you coming from the back? Did you leave something?"

He quickly answers, "Ahh...no...just coming from the restroom," then changes the subject, "Hey...have you heard from Tom lately? I haven't seen my man in what, a week now, right?"

Pausing before answering, she still eyes Val as she passes by, then finally says, "Yeah, it's been a week, and I haven't heard a damn thing from him, either. It's startin' to piss me off! I'm tempted to call the police."

Rod shrugs and says, "Wow…I don't know what to tell you. He still might turn up, believe it or not."

"He better—if he cares about his job! He needs to call me and let me know what the hell is goin' on!"

He throws his hands up and replies, "Hey, I feel ya…I guess he doesn't care."

Shaking her head in disgust, she asks, "Anyway…I guess I'll see you tomorrow night, right?"

"Of course, you know I'll be here," then gives a little wave and strolls out of the club as she looks on.

The next night, Ranetta's in the front lobby of the club filling out a missing person's report with the police. Rod's at the bar taking care of customers as usual. After serving a couple, he takes their money and walks back toward the cash register, counting it. Suddenly, he stashes some of it quickly into his pocket, then puts the rest in the register. All the while, a huge old speaker starts to shake and vibrate on the shelf above the register. Though the band's playing on stage, the vibrations of the music don't match the movement of the speaker. Shaking uncontrollably now, it's getting dangerously close to the edge! Rod reaches down below the bar to get a stack of napkins and places them on the counter above. He gets distracted when the MC introduces Val on stage. Looking back, he lays his hands flat on the counter. Suddenly…*bam! Crash!* The bulky speaker comes crashing down, crushing both of Rod's hands! He screamed a scream so loud that the music instantly stopped, as well as all the chatter throughout the club. People around the bar rush to his aid. A guy strains, lifting the heavy speaker just enough to free Rod's hands. He falls to the floor in complete agony. Suddenly, out of nowhere, there comes a chilling evil laughter from the back of the club. People look in that direction with shocked expressions on their faces, wondering, who the hell could be laughing at a time like this! Marco rushes from the DJ booth and exclaims, "Damn…who the hell's laughing! This ain't funny!"

People continue to stare in that direction. Suddenly it stops. He immediately continues to the back to investigate. Ranetta quickly approaches the bar to see about Rod. "Oh my god…what happened?"

The bystander who lifted the speaker answers, "All I know is this big-ass speaker came crashin' down out of nowhere and lands on my man's hands."

Another bystander in the crowd whispers to someone, "Uh-oh… lawsuit."

Ranetta happens to overhear it, frowns, and rolls her eyes, then smacks her lips as she says, "Oh lord! How the hell did a big speaker like that get up there in the first place? Oh my god, Rod! I'm so sorry! Did someone call the ambulance?"

One of the servers says, "Yes, I did. They're on the way."

Marco returns to the bar. "I didn't see anyone back there. That's very odd!"

Ranetta looks at him strangely and asks, "Odd? What's odd?"

He exclaims, "There was somebody laughing back there… laughing at what just happened to Rod."

"Well…let's not worry about that now, Marco. We need to get him to the lobby." So he and another guy help Rod up, then make their way to the front entrance to wait on the rescue to arrive.

A week later, Ranetta gets a double shot of bad news! It seems that one of the bystanders who whispered, "Lawsuit…" was right. Rod filed two days after the incident, citing an unsafe workplace, and also filed for workman's comp because both of his hands were in casts. The other bout of bad news came from a disturbing newspaper article concerning Tom's disappearance. In short, it stated that the body that was found in the big fire two weeks ago could very well be his remains. The final autopsy report will come out within the next week.

"So it's just one thing after another, huh? I don't get it! What the hell was he doin' in that place anyway?" exclaims Ranetta. She hands the newspaper back to Marco.

"It's just speculation, Netta. It's not definite yet."

"Okay…even so, the very fact his name is mentioned is strange in itself."

Marco states, "True, but you did file a missing person's report shortly after it happened, right?"

"Yes! What does that have to do with anything?"

"Well, you know how the press is sometimes…they probably… well…you know conveniently linked Tom into it all."

She looks at him, shocked, and blurts, "What! They don't just conveniently do anything like that, Marco!"

He disagrees, "Yes, they do! Yes, they do!"

"I don't buy it." Still defending his opinion, he says, "He could still turn up out of nowhere."

She shakes her head in disagreement and says, "Yeah, yeah… Rod had the same attitude, but frankly, I feel all of this will turn out to be true."

He shrugs and replies, "We'll see, Netta."

"Yeah…we'll see in a couple of days, Marco."

Two days later, Ranetta leaves her exercise class, jumps into her Benz, and gets on the main road. While driving, she decides to stop at a convenience store. Grabbing a few items, she spots the day's paper and picks it up too. The headline on the front page catches her eye. A sinking feeling comes over her as she reads it: ALLEGED MAN FOUND IN THE LAKE STREET BUILDING FIRE IDENTITY HAS BEEN CONFIRMED. After paying for her things, she quickly walks out of the store and jumps back into her car. She sits there for a minute, reluctant to read any further. She throws the bag into the passenger seat. Eventually, having to know, she reaches into the bag and grabs the paper. Seconds later, as she read more, tears start to flow.

The following weekend, Ranetta decided not to open the club; instead, she and the entire staff paid their respects to Tom. There was a small funeral at a church not too far away from the Wall. To everyone's surprise, Rod showed up with casts on both hands to pay his respect.

The next day, Ranetta's in her office piddling around, trying to take her mind off all that's happened. Of course, the club probably wasn't the best place to do this. She eventually walks into the storage room and, to her disgust, comes upon a foul odor, as well as condom wrappers all over the floor. Locating a broom and dustpan, she starts to sweep. After cleaning up and spraying the room down with air freshener, she pulls down a storage bin from one of the shelves against a wall, then rummages through it. She comes across Ben's old journals, the ones she found just before Arleen died, then decides to take a seat and read one. Page after page, she becomes more intrigued and at times totally gasping in shock! Upon completing the journal, her eyes bulge as she looks up in complete astonishment.

It's the following Saturday night, and the Wall is slightly deserted. Val finishes her set and walks off stage. Ranetta, who's sitting at the bar, gets her attention and waves her over. She takes a seat beside her, then asks, "Hey, Netta…how's it goin'?"

Before answering, she clears her throat, then says, "Well, I must say things could be better these days. I need to ask you a couple of questions. First, I suspect you have slipped back into your…umm… nasty habit. Is this true?" She quickly puts up a finger before Val could answer. "Secondly, why here *of all places*?"

Shocked by the questions, Val hesitates before answering, "Well…umm…you know this is really embarrassing. I don't know what to say."

Ranetta immediately snaps, "Just tell the truth, Val!"

She pauses again, then closes her eyes and finally says, "Okay, okay…Yes! I've been doin' my hustle! I just need to make some extra cash, that's all!" Ranetta drops her head in shame. Tears begin to flow as she continues to explain, "It was only gonna be for a short time. I'm sorry, Netta! If you want me to leave and never come back, I'll understand."

She quickly answers, "No! I don't want you to leave. I just want you to stop! The main reason I wanted you to sing here was to give you a chance to grow. I feel…I at least owe that much to my sister."

Val wipes the tears away as she replies, "What does my mom have to do with anything? She's long gone, Netta. You don't owe her nothing!"

She quickly answers, "Hey…I think I do, Val! I mean with the way your father—"

Val interrupts, "Don't you mention him! I don't want to hear nothing about him! Okay?"

Ranetta's eyes begin to water as she answers, "Alright, alright…I won't mention him again, but he did treat you and your mother wrong—very wrong!"

Val stands, continuing to wipe the tears away, then asks, "Is that all you wanted to know, Netta?"

"Yes, that's it for now, but please don't be sad, okay? I'm sorry for dredging up the past…It's just that you're too talented for it all to go to waste!"

Val quickly says, "It's not *all* going to go to waste, Netta. You'll see! I'm goin' now…I'm tired, and I've got a long day ahead of me." She quickly waves and starts to walk away as

Ranetta says, "Alright, I hope you're right. I really do. Please… take care of yourself!" Val rushes to the entrance and disappears out the door.

Another week rolls around, and the Wall is jumping again! Ranetta's up front conversing with the new manager while the new bartender is busy serving up the partygoers at the bar. Val…well… she's in the back serving up her pimp, Theo! While he's enjoying himself, she's preoccupied with the bullet hole, now suddenly feeling an evil presence just beyond the wall, again. Once he's done with his business, she quickly gets herself together then tells him, "Hey, baby, I'll be back. I gotta go freshen up a bit before I go on stage."

Smiling crazily, he nods as sweat poured down his face. Val walks out into the dark hallway and quickly scans the area on the other side of the wall…nothing! Back in the room, Theo locates some paper towels and wipes the sweat from his face. He stops momentarily, feeling that something was behind him, turns slowly around. He looks toward the wall where the bullet hole was. Puzzled, he moves closer. Suddenly, "Psst!"

He stops, then smiles as he says, "Awww, damn! You kinky bitch!" He quickly unfastens his pants and unzips. On the other side of the wall, a large pair of hedge clippers slowly rise in front of the hole. Theo, with his pants bunched at the knees, makes his way toward the hole and says, "Yeahhh, ho! I want you to slob my shit down!"

Just before he inserts his penis into the hole, the clipper's blades open! He shoves it in and yells, "Here it is, ho! Do that shit!" At that very moment, *snip!* A bloodcurdling scream erupts from behind the wall, resounding throughout the whole club! His body falls backward as blood squirts everywhere! Hitting the floor with a thud, Theo screams and moans in complete agony. He begins to shake and shudder uncontrollably as he goes into shock.

Meanwhile, the manager, Ranetta, and security guard rush to the back to investigate. Glenn flips on a light switch in the hallway to discover the horrific scene outside the storage room. "Damn, what's that?"

Ranetta replies, "They're hedge clippers! Who would bring those in here, not to mention, how did it get past us?"

Glenn says, "No, not those. What's that?" He points at Theo's severed manhood on the floor in a small pool of blood. They all take a closer look, and Ranetta gasps and exclaims, "Oh my god…Is that what I think it is?"

Glenn sighs loudly, then pauses for a moment before answering, "Yeah…it sure looks like it."

All the while, the manager goes to the storage room door and opens it. She looks inside and screams! Startled, Glenn and Ranetta run to her side to witness Theo's body lying limp in a large pool of blood on the cold floor. Grimacing, Glenn shouts, "Holy shit! Damn, what a way to go!" Ranetta immediately turns away from the sight, and she and the manager embrace each other for comfort.

Val walks up in the middle of the confusion, looking around, wondering what was going on. "Hey, Big G, what's going on?" She peeks around him then screams!

Glenn grabs her close as she yells, "Oh my god! Theo! What happened! Who did this!" As he comforts her, a large crowd gathers outside the storage room. All were trying to get a glimpse of the tragic scene, then someone yells out, "Call 911!" That was the end of Theo Haze, but at the hands of who?

The Investigation

That evening, as the investigators cleared and taped off the area then took all the necessary pictures, Glenn, Ranetta, the manager, and Val gave their statements to the detectives. Though Val was a total wreck, they seemed to drill her the most.

"Like I keep telling you guys, I don't know what happened to him! When we finished taking care of our business, I went to the restroom to freshen up. I come back, and there he is—dead!" She breaks down again.

One of the detectives says, "Okay, okay...so you were in the restroom during the time Mr. Haze was attacked. Does anyone you know have it out for him?"

Sobbing, she answers, "I don't know of anyone in particular. All I know is that someone murdered him very viciously."

The other detective quickly says, "Yeah, and we plan to get to the bottom of it! My suggestion to you is to stay in town and keep yourself available for any more questions."

Ranetta makes her way over and interjects, "Yes...and find a good lawyer in the meantime," as she shoots a stern look at the detectives as they shoot stern looks back at her. The first detective flips his pad and places his pen in his jacket pocket, then says, "We're done here for now. We'll be in touch. Oh yeah...umm...you're gonna have to shut it down for the rest of the night so we can conclude our investigation, Ms. Gibbs. I would take heed of your own advice and get a lawyer, too."

Both detectives smirk at one another, then leave the scene as the other investigators continue their work. Ranetta, Val, Glenn, and the manager just look on in total disgust.

Two days later, the detectives call in Ranetta and Glenn. They're shown the surveillance tape confiscated the night of Theo's murder. One of them points out something on the tape, "See...here's Ms. Tucket leaving the storage room."

Glenn interrupts, "Ms. Tucket? Her last name's Tucket?" puzzled, as he looks at Ranetta.

The detective answers, "Yes! Yes, it is...anyway as I was saying, she walks out then goes straight to the restroom then...everything goes fuzzy after that. Why?"

Ranetta shrugs and says, "I haven't the slightest clue. Maybe the tape ran out...I don't know."

Shaking his head, Glenn explains, "Well...I am in charge of security, and it's my responsibility to monitor the tape, but due to all the commotion, I never got a chance to check it."

The other detective's cell phone rings, and he exits to answer it. "So...is there someone else besides you two that can gain access to the tape?"

Ranetta answers, "No, not that I know of."

Glenn adds, "No one."

The detective, frowning, ponders for a moment before replying, "Okay, but something happened to the tape. As you can see, it's like a portion of it has been erased. I wanna know what was going on while Ms. Tucket was in the restroom." Glenn now notices the fuzziness has disappeared on the monitor and spots himself pointing at something.

He exclaims, "Look, there is something else on the tape!"

The detective looks around and replies, "Alright...I see that you and Ms. Gibbs are right there jolly on the spot. The murder weapon is on the floor. Funny thing, though...when we dusted it down, we couldn't find any prints. Nowhere! Come to think of it...the only prints and DNA of any kind we did discover matched hers!" He points at the screen just as Val appears. Glenn and Ranetta look at each other in shock!

The investigation lingers on for a couple of weeks. Val was called in for questioning several more times until she had enough and hired an attorney. The harassment stopped immediately. They couldn't find any concrete evidence to convict Val with the murder. Neither Ranetta, nor Glenn, could be charged with anything. The investigation eventually came to an abrupt halt. Yet...another mystery is left in the balance within the walls of the old club.

The Beat Goes On

A month later, the Wall was reopened, and surprisingly, business went back to normal! In fact, it increased! Some have speculated that it was because of the now dark history. Seemingly a weird notion, but yet it was a fact! It's a packed Saturday night, the DJ was playing the tunes that moved the crowd, and the drinks were flowing continuously. Everyone was enjoying themselves in the stuffy, smoke-filled club. Val walks in and heads straight for the back, anxious to get on stage. She hasn't sung since the investigation. Ranetta and Glenn are talking as she passes by. They wave at her as she continues to the back to get ready. Ranetta kinda glares at her as Glenn is saying, "Wow, I still can't believe that's Benny's daughter. I just simply never knew. Oh…and by the way, I read that journal you gave me—creepy! To think that Voodoo Child at one point was linked to Ben's murder and now finding out they're one and the same is totally bananas!"

Turning her attention back to him, she replies, "See…I told you that you'd be shocked after reading it. I still don't know how I feel about Val, and I never mentioned this before, but I think Tom had something to do with his murder. It's just a feeling I have."

Kind of baffled, Glenn asks, "Damn, what makes you think that?"

"Because he was hell-bent on searching for money he thought Ben was hiding. He was snoopin' around here and obviously at that other building. Tom was obsessed and quite bitter at Ben for never payin' him back. To think of it, so was Arleen!"

Glenn blurts, "Whoa…you've never mentioned that about her, either! Do you think Arleen knew something and maybe that's what really led to her death?"

Ranetta shrugs and answers, "Could be…I didn't think it at first, but it all starts to make sense now."

Glenn ponders for a moment, then says, "Yes, it does. Someone physically had to be present to spook her so bad that she would have a heart attack."

"Yeah…and I remember Tom was at the doorway when I ran out of the office after hearing the screams. He's the one that ran over to her and felt for a pulse."

Glenn says, "Man, I couldn't make it to work that night. All I got the next day was bits and pieces of what happened."

Exhaling deeply, Ranetta then says, "It all really doesn't matter now. Both are gone, and there's no need stressing over frivolous details. We just have to put it all behind us."

Glenn nods in agreement and replies, "You're right! I think the worst is behind us, and the beat goes on."

True, the beat does go on, but not like either had thought! The next night, one of the detectives from the previous case drops in to visit Ranetta. They sit down and talk in her office. He begins, "So we meet again, Ms. Gibbs. How've you been?"

Smirking, she replies, "Okay, Detective…I know you're not here to see how I've been, so what's this all about?"

"First of all, I was going through some records recently and discovered that Tom Northberg used to work here."

"Yes, he was the manager here."

The detective continues, "Alright…second of all, as you know, he died in that fire down the way two months ago."

Ranetta quickly interrupts again with frustration in her voice. "Yes! So…what's your point?"

He clears his throat and answers, "My point is, Ms. Gibbs…the fire isn't what killed him. A knife in the heart did! More was revealed from the autopsy to prove his death occurred prior to the building going completely up in flames, which leads me to believe that there was definitely foul play involved. In conclusion, did anyone have it in for Mr. Northberg? I can't prove it now, but I think there might be a link between his murder and Mr. Haze's."

She just sits in shock for a moment before answering, "Wow… this all comes as a complete shock! I can't think of anyone wanting to harm Tom in any way. He got along with everyone, except…well, Benny Tucket."

The detective asks, "You mean the old owner?"

"Yes."

He shrugs and says, "Oh, well, that does us no good. He's been dead for a long time now. Unless…there's someone to avenge his death. You know, someone like his daughter maybe?"

This statement really throws her for a loop. She slumps back into her seat, totally mystified.

Could Val really be involved somehow?" she thinks. Her mind races as all suspicions come flooding back.

Meanwhile, just when you thought Val changed her ways after Theo's death, she's up to her old tricks—literally! An old client named Rod, to be exact! Yes, Rod, with both hands bandaged up. After taking care of business, she assisted him with pulling up his pants.

"Hey, baby…umm…I got a little sumthin', sumthin' in one of my pockets for you."

He laughs as she reaches in and pulls out some money.

"Oh, thanks, baby! Here, let me help you fasten up." She reaches down again and buttons his pants, then zips them up.

He nods and asks, "Cool…so, ahh…can I holla at cha tomorrow night?"

She smiles and says, "Hey…if you got the loot, you can knock the boots!"

"I like that. That was cute," he replies, laughing. "Okay, okay… we need to go, though. I'm not supposed to be in here." She nods her head toward the door. They walk up to it, and she quickly motions for him to stop. "Peek outside to see if the coast is clear."

He opens the door and sticks his head out to take a look, then immediately ducks back inside. "Whoa…Ranetta just walked into her office with someone."

Val puts up a finger as they pause for a moment, then she cautiously opens the door. She peeks out, and the hallway is empty. They ease out of the room, and instantly Rod gets a chill! He gazes frantically over both shoulders. Nothing! Suddenly spooked, he hurries along, leaving Val behind. He never looks back as he makes his way out of the club. Val looks at him, bewildered by his actions. She peers back into the hallway and obviously sees nothing. Shrugging and shaking her head, she slowly but surely makes her way out of the club.

Later on, at closing time, Glenn bids the bartender, waitresses, and the rest of the help staff goodbye as they leave the club. He locks the door, turns, and walks past the DJ's booth as he says, "Yo, Marco, my man…you ready to go yet? I'm going to the back to see what's up with Netta."

Marco, who's sweeping up, stops momentarily and says, "Yep, just about done here. Oh, yeah…umm…Gee, can I ask you something right quick?"

"Yeah, what's up?"

Putting the broom aside, he answers, "So what's up with that detective that rolled through here tonight? I thought the investigation was over?"

Glenn shrugs and replies, "Hell…I thought it was over, too. I didn't even notice one had come in here tonight."

"Oh…well…hey, it's no big deal. I was just curious, that's all. I'll be up front when y'all come out."

"Alrighty then…we'll be out in just a minute."

A second later, Ranetta appears from the back and blurts, "I'm ready!"

Glenn looks back at Marco and says, "Well…maybe not in a minute."

Chuckling, he turns back to her and asks, "So do you have everything?"

"Yep, I've got everything, and I'm ready to get!"

Glenn smiles and says, "Cool! I understand that a detective came in here tonight to talk to you?"

"Yep…I'll tell you about it later, though. It's too disturbing to talk about right now." With a surprised look on his face, he asks, "Wow…it's not that bad, is it?"

She looks up at him and says, "In short, let's just say that all of my suspicions pertaining to Tom and Val are back."

"Oh, really? So what, he thinks she had something to do with what happened and—"

Ranetta interrupts, "Something like that, yeah."

By this time, Marco overhears the conversation and interjects, "Something like what? I noticed that detective rollin' up in here tonight. Did he find anything new or just snoopin' around again? Did they really find any money?"

Ranetta and Glenn look at each other, then she answers, "Where did *that* come from? Money? He didn't mention anything about money! In fact, he didn't even talk about the last case. He talked about Tom."

Marco blurts, "Tom?"

She smacks her lips and quickly answers, "Yes, Tom! Can we talk about this some other time? I'm ready to leave!"

Glenn agrees, "Yeah, yeah…sorry! We can rap about all this later."

Looking awfully silly, Marco agrees as well, and they strolled out of the club as Glenn locked the door behind him.

The next evening, at the club, Val enters and eventually spots Rod sitting at the bar. She makes her way over and whispers something in his ear. He gets up and follows her to the back. Premier is jamming on stage, moving the loud crowd of party-goers. They snake their way through while Val lead, tugging on Rod's arm. Now in back, she turns to him and says, "Hey…I've gotta go see Netta about my schedule next week. Go inside and shut the door behind you. I'll be there in a minute, okay?"

He puts up a bandaged hand, acknowledging her, then turns and disappears into the storage room. Val goes to her office, knocks on the door, enters, and closes it behind her.

Rod waits patiently as he sits on a stool. Soon…he notices something different about the room from the night before. The old door that was leaning on the wall across from him has been moved over. Now revealed was Ben's old safe with its door slightly ajar! Knowing nothing was in it, Rod still decided to be nosy and take a peek anyway. He walks over and opens the door, then looks inside. In the back of the safe was a small hatch door slid to one side exposing a red button. Curious, he reaches in and pushes it. There's an instant low buzzing sound followed by a loud click. He looks around and a hidden door opens, slightly. Puzzled, he frowns and walks over to it, noticing frost seeping into the room. He opens the door, and to his great surprise, it was another entrance into the beer cooler! Stepping in, he glances around at all the familiar things like the keg rack, cases of beer and water stacked up along the wall in front of him. The only thing that was unusual was the cluttered mess of mixed cases farther down the wall now are stacked neatly to the side, revealing a trap door with a padlock on it. Rod approaches the door and inspects the lock to find that it was unfastened. Managing to remove it, he opens the door and peeks inside. He witnesses a flight of stairs going down into the darkness. Meanwhile, the rack with the heavy kegs begins to vibrate violently! He whirls around, and the vibrating stops. One of the kegs continues to whirl a bit before becoming completely still. Spooked, he closes the trap door and locks it. He heads back to the storage room when suddenly…"Ppsstt!"

Jumping slightly, Rod turns and screams out, "Who's there?" Unfortunately…he pauses in front of the keg rack, which immediately comes crashing down on him! Not even having time to scream as the full, heavy kegs crush him. He doesn't die right away, but after the mystery door closes and the temperature is mysteriously turned down to freezing, it doesn't take long for him to freeze to death.

A short time later, Val steps out of the office and quickly makes her way toward the storage room. As she approaches the door, it mysteriously locks! She reaches to turn the knob; it won't budge, and she runs into the door. Confused, she starts knocking frantically, looking back all the while, making sure Ranetta doesn't walk out and catch her. Frustrated that her knocks are unanswered, she abruptly walks off just as the office door opened behind her. As she makes her way toward the entrance, she scans the whole club looking for Rod. Pissed, she eventually storms out. Minutes later, the bartender runs out of the beer cooler in sheer panic, motioning for Ranetta, Glenn, and some of the other staff to come to the cooler.

The Investigation

The Wall is swarming with police, and the two detectives that have become very familiar faces are now in the security booth with Ranetta and Glenn, viewing tape. They're trying to make sense of yet another tragedy. The coroner removes the body just before the media arrives. One of the detectives points out to Glenn, Ranetta, and the other one, "See…nobody goes into the cooler between the hour the body was found. Okay, now look at the screen. Mr. Baines is walking into the club at 11:37 p.m. He goes directly to the bar, sits, and orders a drink. Five minutes later, here comes this lady who whispers something in his ear."

Ranetta interrupts, "That's Valencia Tucket."

The detective lifts his eyebrows and continues, "Oh, really… anyway, they get up and stroll to the back. Now on this screen, it shows them stopping momentarily in front of the storage room door. She says something to him, then he walks in and closes the door. She walks over to your office, knocks, then enters and shuts the door behind her. Now it's exactly 11:47 p.m. Ms. Tucket walks out of your office and attempts to open the storage door and ends up running into it because it's locked. She pounds on the door now, looking back in the direction of your office. It seems as though she doesn't want you to know something, Ms. Gibbs."

Ranetta answers, "Yeah, she's been instructed not to go in there anymore. I told her, specifically, that if I caught her in there with someone, I would have her thrown out of here."

The other detective blurts, "Huh…seems some people don't change no matter what the circumstances are!"

Ranetta quips, "Guess not!"

The other detective continues again, "She eventually leaves the club as you can see." He points at the first screen. "Nobody else goes in or out of the storage room between the hour the body was found. So my final question is…how the *hell* did Mr. Baines get into the cooler? The bartender found the body at 12:01 a.m. under the massive heap of kegs. He certainly didn't enter through the cooler door."

While everyone pondered on that question, suddenly the other detective noticed something on one of the screens. "Hey, who's that going into the storage room at 12:08 a.m.?"

The tape is rewound, and they take another look. Glenn exclaims, "That's Marco, our DJ!"

Marco happened to still be in the club when the detective who discovered him on tape approached and asked, "Excuse me, Mr. Edison…could we have a word with you please?"

Marco accepts, then the detective escorts him to the security booth. Now seated, the detective asks, "Why were you going into the storage room at 12:08?"

He answers, "I was looking for some equipment. I thought I put it back there."

The detective crosses his arms and asks, "So during the chaos, all you thought about was getting some equipment?"

Immediately raising his hand, Marco replies, "No-no, sir! I was outside smoking a cig around 11:45, then I came back in at 12:07 and went straight to the back. The music was still blasting and people dancing. Honestly, I didn't even know what was going on at the time!"

The detective hesitates for a second before responding, "Welp…I see you came out of the room at 12:16 empty-handed, so I guess you didn't find what you were looking for."

He replies, "Nope…I remembered I'd left the EQ I was looking for in my car."

The other detective asks, "Okay…so if we go to your car right now, we'll find it?"

He answers, "Yeah…if it's not in the back seat, it's in the trunk still in the box." Then he pulls out his car keys and dangles them in the air.

The detectives look at each other, and one says, "Never mind about that, Mr. Edison. That won't be necessary…Actually, it doesn't matter anyway. Our main focus should be on that storage room. Mr. Baines had to have a way into the cooler from there. After all, they are adjacent to one another. So no more questions right now. If you people would sit tight for just a little bit longer, we'll be finished shortly."

Ranetta quickly asks, "So wait…do you think that what happened was intentional or just another freak accident?"

He answers, "See…that's just the thing, Ms. Gibbs. We can't answer that right now. Not until we gather all the clues and facts we need to solve this case." Both detectives now leave the room.

Marco, ticked, blasts, "Damnn…how are they gonna sit up here and straight interrogate me like that? I didn't do nothing!"

Glenn replies, "Hey, man, they're just doing their job. Don't sweat it…"

Marco interrupts, "Yeah, but you know what, Netta touched on something…It was a freak accident! None of us are guilty of anything!"

Glenn answers, "I truly agree with you, but let's all just chill and stay out of their way. The faster they can come to that conclusion, the better off we'll be."

Marco quips, "Yeah…and the faster we can get the *hell* outta here!"

Ranetta, confused, states, "Damn…yet another person dies up in here! This is all crazy! I feel like this place is cursed!" Suddenly, all the lights in the club go out!

Strange and Twisted

Days later, the authorities concluded that it was a freak accident. They found the safe, the secret button, and the hidden door. It was all much to Ranetta's surprise. She didn't have a clue that such a door was ever installed. She couldn't understand why Ben would do such a thing.

Could he really have been stashing money away somewhere secretly? she thinks. *What was the real purpose for it all?* Mentally exhausted now, she decides to turn in for the evening, at first finding it difficult to sleep, but eventually her mind rests, and she falls into a deep sleep, then begins to dream.

Ranetta walks into the club talking on her cellphone. She gets into it with Ben. He hangs up on her, and she gets pissed and throws the phone into her purse. Now about to flag down the bartender, she's interrupted by someone, "Hello, Netta...what's going on?"

She turns to speak, "Oh...hey, sis! Your goddamn husband's trippin' again! He just called me out of my name and hung up on me, bastard!"

Her sister replies, "Don't worry about him. I'll go back there and take care of it, okay?"

"Umm, okay...but do you need some help? Because, I'll sho' 'nuff come back there with you!"

As she starts to walk away, she nonchalantly says, "Oh no, I got this!" smirking slyly, as she continues toward the back of the club. Shortly after, Ranetta goes to the ladies' room to freshen up.

Meanwhile, her sister hovers in the darkness right outside Ben's office. When Ranetta walks into the restroom, she steps into the light and leans on the wall with her arms spread. Putting an ear to the wall, she listens to what's going on inside. This is at the point when Ben makes the statement, "I know you've come for me. If you do it, trust me! I'll come back…"

Suddenly, she pushes away from the wall and pulls out a gun!

Ben utters his last word…"Me!" then *bang!*

Rosetta Tucket lowers the gun with a devilish grin on her face, turns, and starts to walk away, slowly vanishing into thin air as people begin rushing to the office door. Ranetta jumps from her slumber, sitting up, looking around the dark room, bewildered. *Now what?* she thinks. *That shit was very strange and twisted!*

Her sister's been dead a whole year prior to his murder. After the bizarre car crash that claimed her life, Ranetta had to be the one to positively ID her at the morgue. She knew there was no earthly way her sister could've been the one to kill Ben. So why did her sister's image creep into her dream, she thought. It had to mean something. "If he did have a lot of money, how did he get it?" Suddenly, it dawned on her that personal documents were seized when authorities conducted their investigation after he was murdered. She had a hunch that perhaps he had a life insurance policy on her sister. That could be the very source of the mystery money that's supposed to be hidden somewhere.

It's something worth looking into, she thought.

The next day, Ranetta went to the board of records to look up information regarding the deceased. She found some info on Ben and her sister. It appears he did take out a life insurance policy on her. Supreme Life was the company, and the policy was worth $250,000. He received a check for the full amount two weeks after her death. She now had a sinking feeling that maybe her sister's demise wasn't just an accident.

This might explain how he was able to purchase that other building! she thinks. "Speaking of which…all that business about Voodoo Child and dabblin' in the occult doesn't help his case either! Why would he pose as a crazy old witch doctor slash novelty shop owner by day and an uptight, cheap-ass club owner by night?" The more she thinks about the whole situation, the weirder it gets. Satisfied with the information she discovered, Ranetta leaves and finds her way to some lunch. For the rest of the day, she was left pondering on Ben's old journals and all their contents. All those crazy, twisted, and oftentimes demonic meanings in his writing. She thinks immediately, *Could the spells somehow be linked to all the freaky things that have been happening at the Wall?* She shakes off that silly notion. Ranetta didn't have faith in all that voodoo hoopla! There has to be a deeper explanation for what's been going on. But what? Two murders, three freak accidents, two of which turned into deaths, and one homicide off-site, directly linked to the Wall. It all adds up to complete chaos! Not to mention total bad luck and hardship for the club. The lawsuit settlement she had to pay out to Rod and old debt she inherited from Ben when he owned the joint. *Complete madness!* she thinks. Exhausted, Ranetta lets go of her thoughts for a moment, cuddles up with her little cat, Chel, and watches television.

The next night at the club, Ranetta tells Glenn about the dream she had. "So what do you make of it, Glenn?" She starts laughing at his facial expression.

He smiles and says, "Well…honestly, I don't know, Netta. It all might be linked to your suspicions of Val. After all, she is your sister's daughter."

"Yeah…well, why didn't I dream she did it then? I don't think it has anything to do with her. I certainly don't feel she would be a cold-blooded murderer like that, Glenn."

Shaking his head, he answers, "Hey…you never know these days. You think you know someone and later, they'll turn out to be totally opposite of what you thought."

"I understand what you're saying, but I really doubt it."

Putting up a hand, he says, "Okay…I guess it was simply one of those crazy-ass dreams. You know, the kind people have all the time. Like me, for instance! I have one of those from time to time and can't explain them, but nevertheless, they happen." Nodding her head in agreement, she replies, "Yep…you're right! That's probably all it was then…a crazy dream."

A crowd begins to form at the door, so Glenn had to cut it short. "Ooh…gotta go back to work, but we'll talk some more later, okay?"

"Yeah…let's do that." They both leave the bar and go in separate directions. She goes to her office and shuts the door.

It was a fair-sized crowd tonight, and Val had the night off. Ranetta decided to catch up on some paperwork when she stumbled across one of Ben's journals. Flipping through it, she gets to the last page. Reading it completely, once again she's puzzled.

Why was he in so much rage? she thinks. *Saying that he's gonna come back and exact his revenge on everyone that did him wrong, then drag them back to hell with him. Huh...a spiteful bastard indeed! That's ironic, because he's caused more pain to everyone else than they did him!* She's referring to the lines that read, "To all of those foes on the following list, hardship will come and all will fall completely at my command! Then their souls will be collected and taken to hell!"

Then she asks herself, "What list? Oh my god...could it be the people that have already died in this place?"

Spooked, she slowly flips through the pages of the other journals that were lying on the desk. Nothing! Confused, she thumbs through them again, analyzing every page. Ranetta goes back to the page she already read, then turns it and finally discovers that a page has been ripped out. There was a small corner piece of paper left from the ripped page. Unfortunately, there wasn't anything on it to give any clues to the names on the list. She abruptly shuts the journal, stacks it with the others, and places them in a drawer of her desk. After locking it, she throws the key into her purse. Ranetta takes a minute to clear her mind, then gets back to work.

It's now closing time, and people quickly vacate the premises. Employees begin to leave one by one. Glenn makes his usual sweep, checking the restrooms, making sure the back entrances are locked and secure. As he walked back to the main area of the club, he notices Marco stuffing his backpack, then getting distracted by something going on, on one of the TV monitors. Without turning his attention away, he picks up his bag, and a book falls out onto the floor. A piece of folded paper slips out of the book and lands just beyond it. Glenn goes over to retrieve the book and paper. Before he catches up to Marco, he reads the title of the book: *Another World: An Insight to the Occult.* Stunned, he unfolds the piece of paper and reads it. Now he looks up, bewildered, as he watches Marco walk out of the DJ booth and make his way toward the door. Glenn folds the paper back up and slips it into his shirt pocket, then yells out, "Yo, Marco, you dropped this!" holding the book up in the air.

Marco sees it, then trots over and says, "Oh…thanks, man! I would've been looking for that!" He takes it and shoves it in his bag quickly.

Glenn asks, "So you believe in all that stuff, man?"

Nonchalantly, he answers, "Nah…just something to read. You know how it is…just curious about what makes other people tick."

He replies, "Umm-hmm…I understand."

Marco says, "Well, anyway…I'm out." He raises a fist to give Glenn some dap.

He responds and gives him dap as he says, "Okay, dude…hold it down."

Marco turns away and heads back toward the front entrance as Glenn looks on with his arms crossed.

Ranetta appears from the back and walks up to him and says, "Hey…you ready to go?"

Turning to her, he answers, "Yeah…yeah, I'm ready."

Noticing his distant demeanor, she asks, "You okay, Glenn? Seems like something's on your mind."

"I'm alright…just that I've discovered something strange about ole dude Marco."

Confused, she asks, "Oh, really…what?"

He explains, "He dropped this book on the floor, and when I went to pick it up to give it back, I noticed the title: *Another World: An Insight to the Occult*, and I also found this." Reaching into his pocket, he pulls out the piece of paper and hands it to her.

Ranetta unfolds it, then reads it and slowly looks up, gazing into space. Glenn eventually, waves his hand in front of her face and says, "Hey…you there?"

She quickly responds, "Yeah…yeah…I'm here! This doesn't make sense at all!"

"Tell me about it."

She blurts, "No, you don't understand, Glenn! How the hell did Marco get this? Why did he get this?"

Confused, he asks, "What's it all mean, Netta?"

She answers, "This is a page from one of Ben's journals. It has the list I was just looking for earlier, and it's unfortunately what I suspected! The people we've known around here that have died—they're on this list!"

Glenn's eyes widen as he exclaims, "What? Damn! I saw the names, but I didn't put it together."

Ranetta begins to tear up as she blurts, "Oh my god, Glenn… Could Marco have something to do with what's been goin' on?"

He comforts her as he answers, "Right now, I don't know what to believe anymore. The messed-up thing is the weak evidence we have. The authorities won't buy it! They're not gonna accept all of this black magic, voodoo shit! I don't know…maybe it's all over."

Ranetta looks up at him sobbing and replies, "No…no, I don't think so."

"Why would you say that?"

She answers in a low, raspy voice, "I really don't want to say right now…I could be wrong."

He gently asks, "Oh my god…you're not next, are you?"

"No…no…I don't want to talk about this anymore. Can we just go? I'm sick of this place for now…this eerie, eerie place!"

Glenn quickly agrees, "Alright, let's get the hell outta here! Let me just turn off everything." He breaks away and turns off the TV monitors, lights, and sets the alarm system, then they both promptly leave the building.

Questions That Need Answers

"I don't know what the hell y'all talkin' about!" blurts Marco.

"Yes, you do…it was in the book you dropped on the floor!" shouts back Glenn.

Marco continues on his rampage, "Hey, I found that damn book! I didn't even know that piece of paper existed!"

Ranetta asks, "Where did you find the book?"

He stalls for a moment before answering, "I found it on the ground one night outside the club."

Puzzled, she replies, "See, none of that jives. The only person who has access to my office is me! I haven't taken any of the journals out of here. They've been here intact as far as I know all along. Who would tear out that particular page and why?"

Glenn exclaims, "Well, whoever did it obviously had intentions of puttin' horrendous spells on folks at this club to cause complete chaos!"

Looking bewildered now, Marco mumbles, "Spells? What the hell?"

Glenn glares at him and says, "Yeah, spells! In a nutshell, that's what all this is about. That and murder!"

Now with a nervous laugh, Marco exclaims, "Dude, I think you're jumpin' the gun here, man! I admit, things have been off the' chain around here, but black magic? Come on…you think someone would actually use this shit to commit murders? You know that's a bunch of BS, Glenn. It may be used to commit a few sins, but not murder."

"Murder is a sin, and yes, it could be a bunch of bullshit, but there's nothing else to point to right now. Speaking of which, there's something that's been puzzling me, though. Weren't you the one that was here when all the locks were changed when Netta took over the joint? I remember being late that day, and she had some personal business to tend to. I called and asked if you could get the keys from the locksmith when he finished and that I would pick them up when I got in."

Now very irritated, Marco snapped, "Yeah, dude! Yeah, I was here! That was many moons ago, and I gave you *all* the keys! Why are you on my ass like this! What, are you some kinda damn detective now, playa? What are you really getting at, huh?"

Glenn exhales deeply, drops his head for a second before answering, "Look, Marco, there's just a lot of questions that need answers, alright? We don't mean to offend you—"

Marco interrupts, "What? You don't mean to offend me? Hell, it's too late for that!"

Ranetta interjects, "It's not that anybody's in trouble here… We're just trying to get to the bottom of all the mystery goin' on in this place, that's all!"

"Okay, so where the hell is Val? She needs to be here to answer some questions, too! Considering, she's the one that spends a lot of time in the back, if you know what I mean! For all we know, she could be the one behind all this shit!"

Frowning at his statement, Ranetta replies, "What does she have to do with this? Besides, she's not doin' that anymore, Marco."

He starts laughing and quips, "Please stop being so naïve!"

"Excuse me…I think you need to watch your tone! What makes you so sure she's still trickin'?"

Smirking, he says, "Cuz people talk. Rod talked. Some of the band members talk—"

She interrupts him by putting a hand up, then drops her head and says, "Okay, okay…I get the picture! I guess I'll have to talk to her again later. In the meantime, could we all just forget about this mess for now please? It's exhausting! Let's try to stick together."

Glenn agrees, "That's fine with me."

Marco shrugs and smugly says, "Yeah, whatever!" then he abruptly walks off, snickering.

"Anyway, it's time to open for business," says Ranetta as she just waves him off.

The two go their separate ways to tend to their duties. Glenn goes to unlock the front entrance. Marco was already heading for the DJ booth to set up for the night. Ranetta makes her way to the storage room, now determined to figure out a way to keep Val out! She rummages through a large, metal toolbox and locates a thick steel chain, then spots a heavy-duty padlock with the key in it. Now with both chain and lock in tow, she walks out of the room. Turning and closing the door, she loops the chain around the door knob and through the handle of the stationary door next to it. She locks both ends of the chain together and takes the key out of the padlock.

Later on that evening, Val shows up ready to perform—in more ways than one, of course. She storms into the office and blurts, "Netta, what's up with the chain and lock on the door?"

Ranetta looks up from her work and says, "The storage room is now off-limits. If you need anything out of there, let me know and I'll unlock it for you."

Smacking her lips, Val then asks, "So where am I supposed to change?"

"Huh, use the restroom. That's what the band uses."

Val mumbles under her breath, "Wow!"

Ranetta continues, "By the way, did you know anything about your father's dealings with the occult?"

Shocked by the question, she blurts, "What the hell! Where did that come from? Like I told you before, I don't want to talk about him! That dirty ole fuck! Please, what's this really about, Netta?"

Floored by her reaction, Ranetta exclaims, "Whoa, whoa! Hey, I didn't mean for you to react like that! I'm sorry!"

Tears stream down Val's face as she continues to lash out, oblivious to Ranetta's last statement. "Do you really want to know why I hate my dad sooo much, huh, Netta?"

She interrupts, "I already know why, Val! He used to beat you and your mother! There's nothing worse—"

Val interrupts, "Bullshit! It was much worse! He used to rape me ever since I was ten! I tried runnin' away twice, but he found me each time! It continued until I was fifteen! Then he put me out on the street! I tried telling Mom, but she never believed me! He pimped me until I ran away with Theo! It was around the time of Mom's death! I know that *slimy piece of shit* had something to do with it, too!"

Ranetta sits completely dumbfounded and numb as she continues to hear her rant.

"You know what...I don't even care anymore! My life ain't shit right now, anyway! So I'll just admit it! I'm the one, Netta! I put that bullet in that old fuck's head! I'm the one who shot through the wall to leave that *monster* in his own blood! I'm the missing link—the other ho in the wall, Netta!" she shutters and cries out uncontrollably, then breaks down.

Ranetta jumps up and runs to her side to comfort her. As she's hugging her tight, her mind races! She rocks her gently as tears started to flow. Now somehow, she felt a presence lurking outside the office door! Seconds pass, and it vanishes.

Meanwhile, Glenn finally has a little break at the front door, so he decides to walk over to the DJ booth and smooth things over with Marco. When he approaches the door, he hears two distinct voices coming from within. One was Marco's. The other was a male voice.

But who? thought Glenn. *No one else sits in the booth other than Marco. No one else could fit!* He puts an ear to the door and listens in. "Okay...now that I've raised your spirit and done everything you've asked of me. I think it's time you uphold your end of the bargain."

The other voice replies, "Marco, Marco, Marco! You absent-minded bastard! You're forgetting the most important one!"

Flustered, Marco exclaims, "Excuse me...but you got everyone! Arleen! Tom! You got umm...umm...Theo! Then the last one, Rod! There is nobody else!"

The spirit blasts, "Think about it, idiot!"

Marco, stupidly asks, "Umm...Ranetta?"

The spirit angrily responds, "No...not that bitch! The other one!"

Marco quickly says, "Oh…Valencia! Okay…hell, you can get her tonight!"

"No…not tonight. I just discovered that she's the sole reason for my immediate demise. I've got something special planned for her ass next week."

Marco blurts, "Next week? Come on, dude! Seriously? I've gotta get my hands on that hundred g's right now! I'm ready to leave this dump!"

The spirit blasts back, "Watch it, boy! I'm the one that built this place! Sure, that bitch changed some things here and there, but nevertheless, it's still my joint, got it?"

Cowering down a bit, he answers, "Yeah, I've got it." There's silence for a few seconds, then Glenn notices the doorknob turning. He jumps back just before the door swings open. Marco steps out, mean mugging him, then bluntly asks, "Can I help you, partna?"

Glenn kind of chuckles and quickly says, "Dude, I just came over to say sorry about earlier. So…is everything cool?" extending his hand to him.

Marco reluctantly shakes it and says, "Yeah…whatever, G. Umm…if you'd excuse me, I'm going to get something to drink before I get back to work."

Glenn steps aside and says, "Sure, dawg…excuse me," shaking his head in disgust as he watches Marco stroll off.

The next day, Glenn calls Ranetta to inform her about what he overheard. She answers the phone, "Hello?"

"Hey, Netta…this is Big G. How are you doing today?"

"I'm doing great, Glenn. And yourself?" He could hear it in her voice that she was lying. "Uh-oh, what's wrong? I can tell that's not the truth."

Exhaling deeply, she begins to explain, "I found out some horrible news last night. Val's got some serious issues that she's dealing with right now, and I don't know how to really help her solve them—if they can be solved! Ben did more than just beat her. He… lord, he molested her and eventually pimped her out! He was more of a demon than I'd ever thought. The real kicker, though, is that she confessed to me she shot him."

Immediately, Glenn says, "Unfortunately, I already know all that now. I found out last night! That's why I'm calling you today."

"What! From who? Did you overhear us talking?"

"No…not you two, but Marco and a voice that sounded eerily like Ben's. I heard Marco distinctly say that he conjured up his spirit and that it was directly responsible for all the mysterious deaths that have occurred at the club, including Tom's."

There's nothing but silence, then Glenn asks, "Hello? Hello? Are you still there, Netta?"

Finally, she answers, "Yes! Yes…I'm still here. I'm tryin' to digest everything you just said, that's all. Oh my god!"

"Yeah, I know…totally freaky, huh?"

She states, "Well, I guess that explains Arleen's heart attack and the whole mystery behind Tom's death."

"Yep, not to mention the reason why the police couldn't find any fingerprints on those hedge clippers. Also the fact that those kegs would all of a sudden collapse onto Rod and kill him. You know what, that so-called freak accident that happened to him before with the speaker was probably done just to get at you! He knew Rod would probably file a lawsuit. Man, he is a goddamn demon!"

Ranetta sits in silence for a few seconds before replying, "That's not all, Glenn. I feel like he definitely had something to do with my sister's death. I'm sure that's what my dream was about."

"Wow! He probably did, Netta. I wouldn't doubt it, but unfortunately, there's nothing you can do now."

"Yeah, I know, but why the hell would Marco do something so vile?"

Glenn exclaims, "For the damn money!"

Shocked she asks, "What money? You mean to tell me there's really been some all along?"

"Apparently, according to that bastard, Marco, it's a hundred thousand dollars."

Puzzled, Ranetta asks another question, "Do you know where?"

"Nope, they didn't talk about all that. All I know is something's supposed to go down next week, something pertaining to Val."

"Like what?"

"Still no details. I know it ain't good whatever it is. I heard the voice say that he found out she was the reason for his immediate demise and he had something special planned for her."

Ranetta blurts, "Oh my god! She's the last name on the list! Glenn, don't you see? She's next...next to *die*!"

Time to Disappear

The very next day, Ranetta's on the phone with Seascape Resorts Inc., checking on the availability of the time-share she owns in Myrtle Beach. It would be the perfect place for Val to lay low. Convinced that her life's in serious danger, Ranetta didn't want to take any more chances. She gets the confirmation and sets the dates, then calls the airlines to book a flight from Missouri to South Carolina. Now that all the necessary arrangements have been made, she decides to give Val a call. There's no answer!

Later that day, after several attempts, she still couldn't reach her. Ranetta's mind drifts back to the last encounter with Val when she admitted to murdering her father, especially the part when she stated her life wasn't shit, as she put it.

Her life…that's precisely what I'm trying to save! she thinks. Frantically, she tries to call one more time.

Finally, she answers, "Hello?"

Ranetta quickly replies, "Hello! Are you okay? You sound like you've been crying."

She answers, "Yeah, not only that, but I'm coming down with a cold. So what's up?"

"Well, first of all, I don't think you should come back to the club—"

Val interrupts, "See, I had a feeling this was gonna happen!"

Quickly, Ranetta explains, "No, it's not what you think! I'm not firing you! I just want you to live, that's all!"

Val's voice clears up a bit as she exclaims, "What the hell are you talkin' about, Netta? I'm not in any danger! Theo's dead, and nobody I've messed with knows where I live. What do you mean, you want me to live? What kind of mess is that?"

"Please calm down, Val, and listen very closely. There's reason to believe that someone's after you. I know it doesn't make sense to you right now, but trust me, it's true."

Val snaps, "Who's after me, Netta? Did you tell someone what I told you? There's no real proof! It's your words against mine!"

Ranetta sighs and answers, "No! No! No! I didn't tell anyone! It's just…well…it's just this person or whatever is out to avenge—"

Val interrupts, "Who in their right mind would want to avenge that demonic piece of shit?"

Quickly she replies, "He would!"

Val blurts, "What!"

Ranetta explains, "Not in the physical sense, but in the spiritual."

She quips, "Oh, come on, Netta. You believe in that crap?"

"It's not so much what I believe, Val. It's just what I know." Hesitating before replying, she says, "I've always known about his alter ego, Voodoo Child, ever since I was little. I used to see all these crazy books with spells and demonic rituals in them down in our basement. I remember there were voodoo shrines and different kinds of candles all over the place, too. All that mess totally spooked me, so I basically stayed away. As I got older, I dismissed it all as nothing but a bunch of hype and BS."

Then Ranetta asks, "So you've known all along he was into the occult?"

She answers, "Yeah."

Ranetta continues, "Well…make no mistake, Val. It's real! That's the reason I'm sending you to Myrtle Beach. I have a condo there, it's a time-share, and I've also booked you a flight. Just think of it as a two-week vacation on me."

Val quickly asks, "Okay…so what happens when I come back? If his spirit's after me, won't it find me there?"

"No…everything seems to be connected to the club. All that has happened has been strictly in the club. The only other incident that's occurred on the outside was at the other building Ben owned."

Val immediately corrects her, "No…you mean the building that bastard inherited from my mom after she died. She owned it first!"

Shocked, Ranetta exclaims, "Huh, what do you mean? My sister owned that building? How in the world...She didn't have the money—"

Val interrupts, "She got it from Uncle Blue when he died. He left a small fortune for her. It was in his will."

"Oh, wow! Unfortunately, I wasn't that close to him due to the fact I had moved away to live with our father after him and Mom got separated" Then she mumbles under her breath, "That's why he did it."

Val asks, "What did you say?"

Ranetta quickly answers, "Oh, nothing...Anyway, your plane leaves in two days. I'll give you enough spending money, don't worry about that. I'll take you to the airport also, okay?"

"Yeah, yeah...okay. I think it's totally weird and a huge waste of time, but whatever!"

Relieved, Ranetta exclaims, "Thanks! Just think of it as a free getaway! We'll figure out what to do next when you get back."

"That's fine...thanks."

Smiling now, Ranetta says, "You're welcome...Now I have to run. Got a lot to do. Call me later please?"

"Alright, I will...bye."

"Bye."

Two days later, Ranetta pulls up to meet Val at a fast-food joint. They'll grab some breakfast before the trip to the airport. As she's parking, her cell phone rings. It's Marco!

"Hey, Netta, just calling to ask if you could get a hold of Val for me? The band...umm...wanted to rehearse some new material with her...umm...maybe tomorrow?"

Coolly, she answers, "Umm...yeah, okay. I'll let her know and call you later."

He kind of laughs, then says, "Cool! I appreciate it. Talk to you later. Bye."

She quickly answers, "No problem. Bye." Then mutters to herself, "This sleazy-ass, conniving, good-for-nothing weasel! Wait until I tell Glenn! But first things first, meet with Val, have breakfast, then head straight for the airport."

Five minutes later, Val shows up with a suitcase in tow. They sit down, order their food, eat, and chat briefly before jumping in the car and heading for the airport. When they arrive, Val checks in her luggage, gets her ticket, and they walk through security. The plane will start boarding in fifteen minutes, so as they're making their way toward the concourse, Ranetta reminds her, "Look…have fun, stay out of trouble, and call me as soon as you touch down."

Sarcastically, she replies, "Okay, Ma! As soon as I touch down… Ma!" laughing as Ranetta rolled her eyes.

"Alright, alright, I get it! I'm not your mother, but all jokes aside though, *please call me?*"

Val nods her head. They hug, then she gets in line to board the plane. Eventually, the passengers begin to move, and she turns to wave at Ranetta. She waves back, smiles, and watches her disappear down the tunnel.

A couple of hours go by, and finally, she gets that call from Val. "Hey, girl! You made it there okay? That's great!"

"Yeah, but why does this dude have a sign with my name on it?"

Ranetta laughs, then says, "Oh, that's your limo driver. Surprise!"

"What? Thank you! I've never ridden in a limo before."

Beaming, Ranetta replies, "Yeah, I know…just another little surprise. He'll take you to the resort and pick you up when it's time for you to come back. Use a cab while you're there if needed. Everything's there at your disposal actually. There's plenty of restaurants, shops and, come to think of it, there's even a mall nearby."

Val chuckles and answers, "Okay, cool! Thanks…Ma!"

Laughing at the crack, Ranetta says, "Okay, so you have jokes, again?"

Now they both laugh, then Val says, "I think you might be right…This will be good for me. I'm starting to feel better already. Thanks, Netta. I really appreciate this. Truly I do!"

Beaming again, she replies, "You're so very welcome indeed. Have a great time, and I'll see you when you get back, okay, lady?"

"Without a doubt, I'll call you later to let you know how I'm doin'."

"You do that. Take care. I love you."

"Love you too. Bye."

"Bye."

Later that evening, Ranetta makes a call to Glenn.

"What's up, Netta? I'm glad you called because I've been seriously thinking about our last conversation and was wondering… what the hell are we gonna do with Val?"

"Welp…first of all, she's been taken care of already. I sent her to a time-share I own in Myrtle Beach. I had to do something fast, Glenn! Secondly, that clown Marco had the nerve to call me this morning lookin' for her. He claimed the band wanted to rehearse some new material, but what the dum-dum doesn't realize is the band's out of town on another gig."

"What? Are you serious? When did he say they wanted to do this?"

"Tomorrow."

Then he asks, "So what are you gonna do?"

She hesitates before answering, "I don't really know right now. I do know this…I don't want to call him."

Bluntly, he says, "So don't. Leave his ass hangin'. He'll get the message, and we'll just see his shiftless behind on Friday."

She laughs and says, "Yeah, that's good! I agree."

"Good! In the meantime, though, we're gonna have to come up with some kinda plan to rid ourselves of this curse. Obviously, letting Marco go won't do the trick."

She quickly adds, "Yeah, it might make matters worse! He seems to be the link to starting this curse, and unfortunately, he might be the only one to end it."

"Yep…true dat, but how in the hell are we gonna convince this money-grubbin' SOB of his wrongdoings, Netta? Deep down, I don't think he even gives a damn about anything except his own personal agenda!"

"Good question, good point. It's not gonna be easy, but we have to at least try."

Flustered, Glenn says, "I know we do…damn! We gotta come up with something fast! Anyway, see you Friday evening."

"Look, don't worry about it, Big G, we'll take care of it. I'll talk to you later, okay?"

"Yeah, okay…Take it easy." Then they hang up.

Straight to Hell

It's early Friday evening, and the club was packed as usual. Glenn's up front patting down patrons as they entered. Marco's pacing the floor outside the DJ booth. The music's blasting, people conversing and dancing all over the place. He stops momentarily, distracted by something in the booth. Now ticked off, he punches his hand, then storms into the booth. The door slams behind him.

"Something's not right! It's like her presence has disappeared altogether!" the spirit bellowed. "What the hell have you done, you stupid jerk?"

Instantly, Marco throws a hand up and exclaims, "Look, damn it! Enough with the insults, okay! I don't know where she is. Just be patient. She'll show up sooner or later. After all, I'm sure one of her tricks called her by now."

The voice blasts, "You're a goddamn clown! The door to the storage room has been padlocked since last week! That bitch Ranetta has shut that down for good around here. What happened yesterday, huh? How come she didn't show up?"

Marco blasts back, "I didn't know she did that, asshole! I haven't been back there!" *Smack!* Marco's knocked off his feet, slamming into the door.

"Watch it, boy! Your ass has been slippin' lately. I have a feeling my cover's been blown. If it has, the gig is up. She'll never come back, and that won't be good at all. Cuz ya see, it won't be pretty around here, especially for *your* ass!"

Marco drags himself up off the floor and stumbles to open the door. He leaves and storms outside as he pulls out a cigarette. Pissed, he paces the pavement trying to calm down as he takes a couple of long hard draws on his cig.

Ranetta pulls into her usual parking space, turns off the ignition, and gets out the car to unsuspecting yelling from across the parking lot.

"Hey! Hey! Netta! Yo, what the *hell* happened to Val yesterday? I thought you was gonna call me!"

She looks at him like he's crazy and yells back, "What the hell's wrong with you? Why are you yellin' like that?"

He takes one last draw on his cig, then plucks it aside and meets her at the entrance. "What's wrong is, nobody showed up. I was waiting out here for a damn hour! I guess nobody feels the need to be professional anymore."

Ranetta turns toward him and blasts, "You need to *chill*! First of all, it's obvious she was unavailable because I didn't call you. So why the hell would you show up anyway? Secondly, the damn band is out of town on a gig. I thought you knew?" Now putting a hand in his face, rolling her eyes, she just smacks her lips as she strolled into the club.

Marco stands there looking stupid with no rebuttal. She greets Glenn in front, "Hey, Glenn, Marco's trippin' again. He needs to calm down and just do his job or go home."

He walks in, and Glenn stops him. "So what's up, Marco? You got a problem?"

He quickly replies, "No...no problem, man. I just need to get back to work. Excuse me."

Then he rushes back to his booth and closes the door. Ranetta and Glenn gaze at each other, then burst into laughter. Glenn gives her a wink as they depart. Marco sits down behind the control board, and just before he turns on his mic, *smack!* His head sails forward, bumping into the microphone. He doesn't say a word. He just gathers himself and carry on.

The night continues without further incident. Ranetta's in her office planning a talent showcase for next week. Glenn scans the club and continues to watch the door. Shannon, the manager, is in the ticket booth counting money. Marco, seemingly depressed, sits with his head in his hands when suddenly the spirit spoke, "Well...where the hell is she? Is she comin' tonight or what?"

Marco replies, "I don't know, Ben. The band's out of town on a gig, and Ranetta hasn't heard from her."

"Bullshit! Something's wrong! That bitch is probably hiding her somewhere!"

"Why the hell would she do that?"

"Because she knows the truth, *fool*."

Marco nervously answers, "No-no…you're jumpin' to conclusions, Ben—"

The voice interrupts, "Let me tell you something, *punk*. If she doesn't show up tomorrow night, it's *not* gonna be pretty!"

"But—"

He's interrupted again. "But, *my ass*! I don't wanna hear it! In fact, speaking of night, you have a good one, ya bastard!"

Smack! Marco's head slams into the control console, then the electricity goes out! The blackout causes the club to close early.

The next night, everything seemed normal, so to speak. The lights were back on, but not without costing Ranetta a pretty penny. The whole entire circuit breaker had to be replaced due to the extensive internal damages. She and Glenn had a general feeling that the spirit was angry. Now pondering on what could happen next, they talk, "This is madness, Glenn! I can't continue on like this. This whole situation is gonna drive me straight to the poor house!"

In total disgust, he shakes his head and replies, "I understand completely, Netta. We've gotta figure out something fast. It's getting very ugly around here."

Then out of nowhere…"You can say that again!" *Smack!* Ranetta's face snaps to one side, and then she hits the floor! Glenn looks on in horror! People that were around did double takes, not believing what they just saw.

One female patron yelled out, "Did you just hit her?"

He shakes his head frantically, too dumbfounded to speak. Another female exclaims, "He had to…There's no one else here!"

Seconds later, an angry mob of females started to gather around. One of them helps Ranetta to her feet when. Menacing laughter ensues, then "Bring that bitch to me!" the voice bellowed over the loud music. The lights begin to flicker one by one and started blowing out! Sparks and glass flew with each blast! Soon total darkness and pandemonium! Everyone's screaming and running for the front entrance.

As the week passed, the burning question on Ranetta's mind was, *Should I open the club for business or not?* There were no more doubts now; they're dealing with an evil force that will stop at nothing to get what it wanted. Considering the club's financial state, though, she had no choice. Thursday comes around, and she calls a meeting at Lovey's diner, a block away from the club. Shannon, Glenn, the bartender, and one waitress show up. Ranetta greets everyone at the door, then they all sit as she begins the meeting.

"I've called you all here today because, as you know, there've been a lot of unexplained disturbances goin' on at the club—"

Glenn quickly interrupts, "Unexplained? Nah, nah, Netta! We don't have to hide what's really been goin' on no more. Ben's evil-ass spirit has been haunting that joint, period! That's what's been goin' on."

The bartender and waitress eyeball each other, then the bartender asks, "Ben? Who the hell is he?"

Ranetta answers, "He was the original owner of the club."

The waitress asks, "What happened to him?"

Glenn blurts, "He was shot! In the club, no doubt!"

Both ladies look at each other again in complete shock. Ranetta quickly adds, "Yes, and that's when the madness followed. You may not believe in the occult, God knows I didn't at first, but I do know something demonic is goin' on around there."

Glenn adds, "Yeah, and that damn rat, Marco, is behind it all!"

Shocked by his statement, Shannon asks, "Marco? Why would he have anything to do with what's been goin' on? I mean, he's just a DJ."

Ranetta replies, "It's a long story, girl. One I don't care to get into right now."

Shannon asks, "So what's the plan?"

"Well, right now we're just gonna go on with business as usual. I've organized this talent showcase that's goin' down this weekend, so we can just focus on that. I need all of you to keep your eyes and ears open for anything suspicious or out of the ordinary, okay? Think safety! If it looks like danger that's about to happen, react quickly please! These are the only things I can think of doin' right now."

Frustrated, Glenn says, "Well, hell...damn it! I guess you're right! That's pretty much all we can do! Our hands are tied right now."

Ranetta replies, "Hey, everything's gonna be alright, Glenn."

"Yeah...we hope."

The next evening, the Wall opened without a hitch. The crowd wasn't as big as the previous weekend, but it became pretty sizeable considering the circumstances. Calvin Kitchen, the club MC and equipment manager, was assisting Ranetta with setting up for the showcase. Marco was supposed to help before the club opened but was late. Glenn shows up a few minutes after he does, of course, because his tardiness was for a reason. He didn't trust Marco anymore, so he was tailing him, watching his every move! When he walks in, he spots Ranetta and pulls her aside to pitch an idea that he had. "How about you tell Marco that Val will be here tonight, you know...to kinda stall the inevitable."

She asks, "The inevitable? What do you mean?"

"What I mean is you already know Ben's gonna probably start actin' a fool tonight, so I figure maybe we could use that to stall 'em a bit. Perhaps then you could get through this event tonight without any problems."

She ponders on his suggestion for a moment then says, "Hey...I guess it's worth a shot."

Later that evening, the MC takes the stage and introduces the first act, a comedian by the name Rudy Taylor, a.k.a. Li'l Rude. As he was slaying the crowd with his jokes, Glenn walks over to Marco to have a talk. "Yo, Marco...umm...Netta wanted me to ask if you could find those tracks that Val was rehearsing to a couple of weeks ago. She's comin' in to do a surprise performance tonight."

Marco's eyes brighten as he smirks, then says, "Oh, really? Alright then. I can do that. When exactly is she comin' in?"

Glenn simply shrugs and says, "I don't know. All I do know is, she'll be here."

Marco nods and makes his way to the DJ booth as Glenn gazes at him for a moment, then he walks over to where Ranetta was sitting. Glenn bends down and whispers in her ear, "Okay, I told him. We'll just wait and see what happens now." She nods at him, and he returns to the front entrance.

Sitting in the booth, Marco searches through his library of CDs, looking for those tracks, when…"Well, is she comin'?" blasts the voice. His body jolts from the sudden raging question from behind him. He quickly answers, "Yes, Yes! She's comin', Ben! They've planned a surprise performance tonight. Now could you tell me where the money's buried, please? I know it's in the basement under the cooler, but where exactly?"

The spirit exclaims, "It's not buried! It's located under a trap door built into the floor. It's been under your nose all along. Of course, I'm not worried about you escaping with my loot now because yo' ass won't make it out of here alive, and that's *if* I don't get what I want. She better show up for your own sake!"

Seconds go by…total silence. Marco finally speaks out, "You still here, Ben?"

There's no answer, so he gets up, opens the door, and peeks out. The comedian is finishing up his set and begins to leave the stage. The audience claps and cheers as Calvin takes the stage again to introduce the next act. Marco takes advantage of the opportunity, but before he leaves the booth, he locates the tracks and sets them aside. He walks out and sneaks his way toward the cooler entrance. Slipping in, he strolls to the trap door inside and pulls out a set of keys from his pocket. He tries two with no success, then with a third, the padlock snaps loose. Pulling the door open quickly, Marco climbs in and locates the light switch. He flips it on, and the dim light illuminates the top of the staircase. He peers down the steps into the darkness below, then closes the door to a crack and proceeds down the stairs. Meanwhile, the showcase continues on, two acts down and two more to go! Calvin announces the third act of the night, a jazz pianist from New Jersey.

As the night progresses, Ranetta looks around the room and starts to relax. *I guess Glenn's idea worked, but for how long? It's not like we can use this lie every night!*

Little does she know, she was so right!

Marco manages to find the briefcase filled with the hundred g's hidden under the trap door like Ben said. He sits it in one of the dark corners of the room, then hurries back to the DJ booth. His plan is to get his backpack later on and stuff it with the money. When he walks into the booth and closes the door, "So where is she?" says the voice.

He answers, "Oh…umm…I'm about to go see right now."

Immediately leaving the booth, he doesn't realize the spirit follows him. Glenn's over talking to Ranetta and Shannon. "So far, so good, huh?"

Ranetta answers, "Yeah…that was a good idea. Of course, I don't think we can keep this up."

"Realistically, no…but we'll worry about tomorrow night and beyond later."

Confused, Shannon asks, "What are you two talking about?"

Ranetta replies, "Yeah, remember at the meeting when we were talking about all the eerie things that have been goin' on around here and that me and Glenn linked it to the occult?" She nods and answers, "Yes."

"And remember how we think Marco's behind it all?"

"Yeah."

"Well, he is. So we concocted this story about Val coming in to make a special appearance so he could relay that to the spirit so as to stall him from causing any mischief tonight."

Glenn adds, "Yep…like I said, so far, so good."

Still confused, Shannon asks, "Okay…so what does Val have to do with this?"

Now all of a sudden, Marco walks up and blurts, "So what's this I hear about Val?"

They all stood there, dumbfounded, then Ranetta quickly speaks up, "Oh…hey, Marco…umm…she's on her way. I just got off the phone with her. Do you have those tracks ready?"

Hesitating before answering, he says, "Yeah, I've got them ready. Is she really comin'?"

With a nervous laugh, she replies, "Of course. Why would you ask me that if I just told you so, silly?"

He starts to walk away as he answers, "Naw…ahh…never mind me," then without hesitation heads for the cooler. In the back of his mind, he thinks, *I better get this loot and hold it close just in case I have to make a run for it!*

Ben's spirit continued to hover around the group. Shannon frowned at Marco as he was walking away and says, "Damn, what's up with him? He's actin' kinda suspicious."

Glenn replies, "Exactly! I'm gonna go see what he's up to."

Before he takes off in hot pursuit, Ranetta says, "Be careful please?" He throws a hand up in response, continuing toward the cooler entrance. Now she turns to Shannon and starts to explain, "Shan, Val's in trouble! Ben's after her! I know it doesn't make sense to you, but her life is really in danger! That's why I sent her to South Carolina two weeks ago. She's still there. It's all complicated, I know, but rest assured it's essential that Marco knows nothing of this, okay? So far, there hasn't been any mishaps tonight, and I—"

Then the voice interrupts in the most vicious demonic tone ever, "Not until now, *bitch*!" *Smack!* Ranetta's body went sailing across the table that was in front of her! Shannon, and the people in the surrounding area start screaming! The artist on stage stops playing and looks on with concern. Chaos starts to brew as the lights begin blinking off and on. Then a whirlwind of evilness ensues! Glass starts popping everywhere! Light fixtures exploded into sparks and fire! Now the panicked crowd is in a frenzy! The huge stampede toward the front entrance cause some to be trampled to death! The fire was spreading fast, and smoke starts to thicken. The sprinkler system finally activates. Shannon struggles to pull Ranetta up off the floor as the smoke makes her gag. Still buzzing from the blow she received, Ranetta manages to muster a little strength to gain her balance, then both stagger to the front entrance. In a whisper, as they were making their way out, she asks, "Wha-wha…what about Glenn?"

Meanwhile, Glenn has followed Marco into the basement. Both are completely oblivious to what was going on in the rest of the club. He stands in the darkness about midway of the staircase, watching Marco in the dim-lit room going for the briefcase. When he locates it, he turns and heads for the stairs but is stopped dead in his tracks!

"Where the hell do you think you're goin'?" bellowed the enraged spirit. Suddenly, a blast of wind blows out of nowhere and lifts Marco off his feet, then he hits the ground with a hard thud! As he was in the air, the briefcase flew out of his hand and hits the wall behind him, popping open! Money flies everywhere, mixing with the whirlwind of dust and air!

Marco gazes up and yells, "My money!"

The spirit laughs and blasts, "Your money? What the fuck you mean, your money? The deal's off!"

Marco immediately stands and shouts, "How the hell do you figure that? Val's on her way…Ranetta said it!"

After hearing that, Glenn could no longer contain himself and blurts out, "You good-for-nothin' sellout!"

The spirit becomes slightly visible now and turns toward him and sarcastically shouts, "Yeah, no doubt!"

Glenn interrupts, "So you do exist! You goddamn devil!"

The spirit screams back, "You damn right, and now you won't!"

A fireball appears in one of its hands, and he lobs it toward Glenn with great fury! It catches him right in the face sending him backward, screaming! He falls and rolls down the stairs, continuing to scream in agony as the flames pierce and fry his flesh! Scrambling with much fear and confusion, Marco picks up the briefcase and starts to scoop up the money. As he's stuffing the case, he exclaims, "I don't understand it! She's who you wanted, Ben!"

Deep down, he knew the truth now. His heart sunk deep. Val was not showing up, and his time was up! What the spirit bellowed next confirmed it.

"The bitch is in South Carolina, you stupid-ass bastard! Now it's time to send you, this money, and this damn place straight to *hell*."

Then the whole room erupts into an inferno!

Marco screams, "Nooo!" as the flames engulf his body! Now the whole place blazes completely out of control.

Hovering outside in an alley adjacent to the club is Calvin, gagging and coughing. When he finally looks up, he notices Ben's spirit a few feet away, witnessing the club being overtaken by the flames.

He cautiously walks over and says, "It appears that you still have some unfinished business, Ben. Welp...I have to tell ya, I found out something that'll suit us both. Do you remember Big Boozy, that son of a bitch that robbed you a long time ago?"

The spirit answered, "Yeah...I remember that clown."

Calvin continued, "The comedian that was here tonight, turns out to be his cousin. He told me Boozy's got a nice-ass club in Atlanta. He must have flipped that money and—"

The spirit interrupts, "So what! You tryin' to be funny?"

"No! No! What I'm tryin' to say is, he needs someone to run it. He's tryin' to expand another business he has, so I was thinking when Ranetta gets the insurance money, I could persuade her to move there to start over. Val would more than likely follow. You get it? It'll be your second chance. Just tell me how to bring you back."

The spirit ponders on this for a second or two, then asks, "So what's in it for you?"

"Well, it seems Boozy is a lot like you. He likes to hide money around because he don't trust nobody. His cousin told me...well, you know how it is when a muthafucka gets drunk, they talk a lot! Anyhow...he told me Boozy's got about a quarter of a million stashed in a secret safe hidden in the club somewhere—"

The spirit interrupts, "Yeah, he claims! That drunken son of a bitch was probably yankin' yo chain!"

"Even so, you'll still get two for the price of one. After all, he did steal from you. With Boozy out the way, there's a chance I can get my hands on that bread, baby."

Then the spirit says, "You'll have to recite a particular phrase from one of my journals, as well as follow some instructions thereafter to summon me. Once I'm back, though, I'm in charge. Got it?"

"Yeah, I got it, but those journals were in Ranetta's office. They're up in flames now!"

He points toward the rapidly diminishing building. "No, she has the one you need in her possession."

Calvin smirks and says, "Cool! I guess I'll see you in Atlanta, then."

"If all goes well, but just know, if you fail me, you *will* meet the same fate as Marco," then the spirit fades completely away.

Firefighters battle the blaze as the police formulate blockades beyond the array of fire trucks and twisted lines of hoses. The media pulls up, and helicopters hover above. The partygoers who fled the scene are joined by other countless spectators lining the blockades, looking on in amazement. In the heap was Ranetta, Shannon, and a few other employees that made it out safely. Ranetta, coughing, turns to Shannon and says, "Oh god...I don't think Glenn or Marco made it out!"

Already crying, Shannon whines, "I don't know...I never saw them come out! Oh god!" She breaks down, and one of the former employees comes to comfort her. Ranetta looks on with tears streaming down her cheeks, then suddenly out of nowhere, she yells out, "Damn you, Ben! You monster! I hope you burn in hell for eternity!"

Brink of a New Beginning

Two days later, the only thing that stands are the sparse charred pieces of metal framing embedded in the cement foundation. There are piles of ash and burnt debris everywhere. The Wall completely burned to the ground in a matter of minutes! Insurance agents are on site, taking pictures to complete their assessment of the damage. The media is also on the scene, again finalizing their report on the tragedy. They are calling it a freak accident, while some speculate faulty wiring and others formulated rumors that it was deliberately set for the insurance money. Nevertheless, the insurance company couldn't proceed until the arson detective gave his final report.

The report comes days later, and the conclusion is a faulty electrical system. The detective couldn't find any traces of accelerants, explosives, extra wiring, or triggers of any kind, so it wasn't arson! He did make a note that the circuit box was replaced, but couldn't confirm whether or not it had anything to do with causing the fire. Of course, he definitely didn't have a clue that it was all purely speculation!

The investigation is finally a wrap, and a check is cut to the tune of $250,000!

How ironic! thinks Ranetta. *The same amount as the life insurance payout to Ben! Could this be poetic justice or what?*

It takes a week or so to determine who the eight bodies pulled out the rubble are. Confirmation finally comes that two out of the eight are Marco Edison and Glenn Johnson. Ranetta decides to have a double funeral. Despite all the evilness Marco was behind of, she finds it in her heart to pay respects by including him.

The funeral is long and sad. A lot more people turn up than expected. As Ranetta is weeping in her seat, a hand laid on her shoulder. She turns to see Calvin smiling at her. He bends down and whispers in her ear, "Can I talk to you later? Lunch is on me?"

She nods at him as she wipes the tears away. He glances over at Val, who's sitting next to her, and winks. She waves at him, then turns her attention back to the service.

Later on at lunch, Ranetta and Val meet Calvin at Lovey's diner. Val's been rather clingy to Ranetta since coming back from South Carolina. As the three feast, Calvin asks Ranetta what her plans were for the future.

"So, Netta, what's the plan now? You gonna start over?"

She pauses a moment before answering, "I don't know, Cal... Starting over...whooo, that's a tough one!"

He quickly says, "Oh, no...I didn't mean any disrespect by that. I was just curious."

"Oh, I know, I know...it's just that I haven't really given it much thought lately. I've been consumed with reporters, insurance companies, lawsuits, and a double funeral. It's been hectic!" Val adds, "Yeah, not to mention, I've been nothing short of a handful, too."

Ranetta quickly replies, "Nooo...no, you haven't."

"Yes, I have! And I'm gonna do whatever I can to help you get back on your feet. That's the least I can do." She smiles and says, "Aww...thanks, Val! I appreciate that!"

Calvin smirks and says, "You know what...I've got an idea for that, if you don't mind hearing it."

Ranetta asks, "Oh yeah? What?"

"Welp...I know this cat down in Atlanta that has this upscale joint called Club Boozy's. He's looking for someone with experience to run it so he can concentrate on developing his other business. It's a uniform, linen sales, and cleaning company. Floyd 'Big Boozy' Clinton is his name. Now I know you're used to runnin' the show, but if you get your foot in the door and more time to raise the necessary capital, maybe you can take off his hands at some point. It's just a thought."

She laughs as she replies, "I don't need to run the show! Managing it, I can do! All that I've been through this year...please...I don't want the responsibility of ownership anytime soon. Actually, though, that does sound good right about now, Cal. A change of pace and a change of scenery! Would you go with me, Val? Maybe you could start singing again."

She beams as she answers, "Wow, of course! I would love to get out of this godforsaken town! When do we leave?"

Ranetta and Calvin laugh. "Slow down! Slow down! We have to make the necessary preparations, first! That's a big move!" Calvin was in agreement, as well as secretly beaming. His devious plan was slowly but surely coming together. They finish their lunch, then say their goodbyes and go their separate ways.

The next couple of weeks were filled with planning. Calvin connected with Floyd, and surprisingly, everything worked out. Ranetta ironed out all her issues and started packing. Val gathered all her belongings and decided to stay with Ranetta before they made their move to Atlanta. When they get there, they've decided to be roommates, at least until they were both on their feet.

Calvin eventually makes a surprise visit over to Ranetta's place. He knocks on the door. Seconds later, she answers. "Oh…hello, Cal! Ahh…what brings you by?"

He slyly says, "Just wanted to see if you needed any help packin'?"

She smiles, steps aside, and says, "Come on in. The more, the merrier! I'd appreciate it."

He walks in and looks around to witness an assortment of neatly stacked boxes taped up, labeled, and ready to go. Fragile goods such as vases, glass statues, and pictures in frames were lined up ready to be wrapped and packed.

"Wow…you seem to be on the ball, already! You sure you need help?"

She laughs and says, "Definitely! My office is still a mess. I have a few empty boxes left, of course, I need more, but they're all in there, which is where I'm going next."

He just shrugs and says, "Okay…let's get to work."

Her telephone rings at that instant, and she excuses herself, then walks into the kitchen to answer it. He finds his way to her office and stands in the doorway scanning the room. It's just like she'd said—it's still a mess! Stacks of paper, books, magazines, and catalogs everywhere! He smirks and kind of laughs, then shakes his head as he puts his hand on his hips. Then eureka!

He spots what looked like an old journal on top of a stack of forms on her desk. Peering back to see if she's still in the kitchen, he finds that she's still jabbering away, so he dips into the room to investigate. Much to his delight, it was exactly what he was looking for! His sneaky ass grabs the journal and tosses it into the trash can next to the desk. He reaches down and takes the bag out of the can and walks to the doorway. He slowly peeks out; Ranetta's still in deep conversation, so without hesitation, he quietly sneaks his way to the front door. Easing out the door, he walks onto the porch. Calvin looks all about, then suddenly decides to hide the bag behind a big bush out front. Quickly, he makes his way back into the house and stands in the front room. Finally, she gets off the phone and rejoins him in the living room. "Sorry about that. Just runnin' my mouth with Val! So where were we?"

He answers, "Your office."

"Oh, yeah...well, let's get to work." He follows her back, and they start packing.

An hour later, Ranetta plops down in her desk chair, exhales, and blurts, "Phew...I'm pooped! That's enough for now. Like I said earlier, I need more boxes, anyway. Thanks a bunch, Calvin!"

Coolly, he replies, "No problem, Netta...umm...I do have to dip, though. I got some things I got to take care of."

"Oh, that's cool. Go ahead please! I'm done for the day. I'll see you later." He gives her a slight salute, and she waves back, then he promptly leaves the room. Before walking out the door, he turns and yells out, "Hey...you gonna lock up?"

She yells back, "I'll get it in a minute, thank you!"

"Alright then!" He walks out onto the porch. Calvin bops down the steps with a smirk, then locates the bag behind the bush, grabs it, and disappears down the street, whistling a happy tune, a tune of deviltry and deceit!

It's now a week later, and everything's set! Everyone has secured their living arrangements. Ranetta confirmed that she definitely had the job at the club. Val will be a featured act from time to time and is considering enrolling in a technical school. Calvin will work at the club also. The moving truck backs up to Ranetta's house, and soon the movers get to work. A couple of hours later, they're on the road! The trio now has a bout of relief, leaving an abundance of misery and grief behind in Kansas City and contemplating starting anew in Atlanta. Unfortunately, little did the ladies know a trap was being set. One more dirty-ass rat to contend with! More deadly encounters, more chaos, more mayhem was around the corner, and they didn't know it. It seems greed will send a man straight to madness and eventually straight to hell! Next stop, Atlanta.

Part 2

A New Beginning

It's Thursday, 8:36 p.m., and the trio arrive in Atlanta, finally after an eight-hour trip. Ranetta, Valencia, and Calvin can soon get some rest. The movers will arrive tomorrow morning at the Westpark Estates apartments in Fulton County, where Ranetta and Val will be roommates. Calvin's place is in Decatur with his cousin, Rodney Clemens, who won't be in town until tomorrow as well, so the three stay in a hotel downtown. The two ladies share a room while Calvin gets his own. Once settled, Ranetta thumbs through a telephone book in search of some dinner. The two decide to get pizza. After giving the order, she calls Calvin's room to see if he wanted to join them. There's no answer.

Twenty minutes pass. There's a knock on the door. "Who is it?" asks Ranetta.

The voice on the other side replies, "Donnie's Pizza."

"Cool...I'm hungry! Did you ever get ahold of Calvin?" blurts Val.

"Nope." Ranetta makes her way to the door with purse in hand. She opens it, then smiles and asks, "Hello, how much do I owe you?"

The delivery guy says, "That'll be $22.35."

She pays him, along with a tip. Val takes the two boxes of pizza and the two-liter bottle of soda. He replies, "Thank you and you have a good night."

Ranetta says, "Thanks, and you do the same."

After he leaves, she picks up the phone and calls Calvin again. Still, no answer. "Man, I hope everything's alright! He's not answering his phone."

"Who knows, Netta. He might be cruising the town. He has people here, right?" chomping down on her pizza. "Umm...this is good!"

"That's true, but his cousin doesn't get back from Florida until tomorrow." Val smacks her lips, after sipping her soda and says, "Oh, well…maybe he just stepped out. Maybe got something to eat, himself."

"Yeah, maybe…Guess that means more pizza for us."

"Yeah…right!" Both ladies laugh, and Ranetta grabs her a piece of pizza. They both kick back, eat, drink, chill as they watch some TV.

Sometime later, Ranetta decides to get some more ice from the machine outside, just down the way. She grabs the ice bucket and leaves the room. As she's walking, she ponders for a minute on whether or not to knock on Calvin's door. She decides not to, figuring he's either not there or she might end up disturbing him. Finally, reaching the ice machine, she lifts the lid and starts to scoop ice into her bucket. On the other end of the walkway, Calvin eases up the stairs and walks to his door. He's oblivious to her presence as he pulls out his key. Ranetta happens to glance in his direction. "Hey… where've you been?"

He's slightly startled but smiles as he looks over and says, "Oh… hey, Netta! I've just been out, you know…had to get a few things."

She walks over to him and notices he had a bag in his hand. "So what did you get? Did you get something to eat?"

"No, I just got a few little knickknacks. I ate earlier…Chinese food."

"Wow…that's a trip! Me and Val were deciding on that or pizza… We chose pizza. There's still a few slices left if you're interested."

Calvin smiles and answers, "Nah, I'm good, but thanks anyway."

She shrugs and says, "Okay…I'm not gonna hold ya. Just thought I'd ask. Good night."

She waves as he says, "Good night." She turns and starts to walk back to her room, then for some reason is fighting back laughter. Calvin doesn't notice this but looks on until she disappears into her room. He smirks, rolls his eyes, and steps into his room and closes the door.

Ranetta chuckles as she strolls toward her bed. Val, with a peculiar look on her face, asks, "What's so funny?"

She sits the ice bucket on the dresser in front of her bed and says, "Whoo…I might be jumpin' to conclusions, but Calvin's a freak!"

"What? Why would you say that?"

"Well, as I was getting ice, I caught him before he went into his room. When I approached him to ask where he's been, I noticed this bag in his hand, and on it, it said Mojo's Novelty and Fun Shop."

Val, puzzled, says, "So? How does that make him a freak?"

"Don't you get it? Don't you get sex toys and other things of that nature from places like that?"

"Yeah…but you can get a lot of other things from places like that, too."

Ranetta quickly says, "Okay, I guess you're right, but it just seems rather odd, but then again he could have gotten souvenirs or something."

"Exactly! You're probably the one that's a freak. It seems that your mind's in the gutta'!"

She starts laughing as Ranetta immediately grabs a pillow and shouts, "Oh, no you didn't!" She tosses it at Val, who tries to dodge the pillow but not in time. She squeals upon impact, continuing to giggle. Now a small pillow fight erupts. As the ladies are having their playful battle, Calvin is in his room contemplating evil! Ranetta didn't have a clue that in the bag was a small assortment of candles that would be used for the ritual to bring back Ben's sinister spirit to wreak more havoc! He pulls out the journal that he creeped from her house from one of the drawers of the dresser. He lays it down next to the bag and gazes at them with a devilish grin and mumbles to himself, "Time to get paid." He gathers everything up and places it all in the drawer, then closes it. He strolls to the bathroom, whistling. After taking a shower, he decides to turn in for the night, to dream about the inevitable, no doubt.

The next morning, Ranetta receives a call on her cell phone. The movers have arrived and needed the address to their apartment. She and Val gather their things and put them in the car. Ranetta asks Val if she'd go and let Calvin know they were leaving while she went to check out. She agrees and goes to his room and knocks on the door. The door opens, and she jumps back in complete shock! "Damn, Calvin! What the hell!"

He was standing there butt-ass naked! He exclaims, "What...it ain't like you haven't seen me like this before! Shit, I'm horny! I got fifty bucks!"

Val blasts, "Look, you know I don't do that anymore! Damn... you're a perv!"

Calvin frowns and blurts, "What...how you gonna come at me like that?"

Val interrupts by putting a hand up and exclaims, "Anyway, we're outta here! The movers are in town. Goodbye!" She storms off as he just chuckles and watches her for a second or two before slamming the door.

Val's sitting in the car now, fuming, when Ranetta approaches and gets in and puts on her seat belt. She stares at Val for a second, then asks, "Whoa, what's wrong with you? You over there just mean-muggin'."

She smacks her lips and blurts, "You were right about Calvin... He is a damn freak! More like a pervert!"

Ranetta, shocked, asks, "What did he do?"

"Never mind, Netta...don't worry about it. Let's just go."

"Hey, do you want me to go up there and set his ass straight?"

"No, I've already checked his ass! Please can we just go?"

Shaking her head in disgust, Ranetta starts the car and says, "Alright." She reaches over and punches the address to the apartment into her navigation system, then they're off.

As they're rolling down the highway, Val knew it was only a matter of time before she had to give in to her secret craving. A craving that only she knew, not even Ranetta! A bad habit she's had since hooking back up with Theo the second time around. The habit being the white powder one sniffs up their nose to get high! The worst part, though, is how she keeps pondering the offer that Calvin proposed to her at the hotel. The fact is, she had to get some money soon. To her, it seems to be the only recourse. Her anger subsided, just to be replaced with sadness.

They pull into the apartment complex and find their way to the leasing office. Chatting with the leasing agent for a moment, Ranetta finally gets the keys. The movers pull up as they walk out of the office. After flagging them down, Ranetta walks over to the truck. "Hello, I'm Ms. Gibbs. Are you Tony?"

"Yes, how are you doing?"

"I'm good...I just got the keys. We're in apartment building 1200. You can follow me. I'm in that tan Benz over there." She points in the direction of the car.

"That's fine. Is it upstairs or down? I forgot to ask you that over the phone."

"It's downstairs, number 1207."

Tony smiles and says, "That's good. We charge a little more if we have to go up."

She smiles and says, "Oh...good then...so what you quoted me over the phone still stands, right?"

"Yep, it still stands."

"Cool...well, follow me."

He nods as she turns and walks back to her car. Val's on the phone; as she gets in, she overhears her saying, "We can set something up tonight. We'll talk about it later. Gotta go. Bye."

She hangs up as Ranetta starts the car. "What you settin' up tonight? I thought you didn't know anybody down here?"

She backs the car out as Val answers, "I don't...that was Calvin. He told me he's set up an audition so that the owner can hear my chops."

"What...I thought you were pissed with him?"

"Yeah, I was, but he apologized. I think he did that to get back on my good side."

Ranetta parks the Benz in front of their building, and before they get out, she asks, "Okay...so what did he do to get on your bad side?"

Val just shrugs and says, "It's no big deal now. I've moved on."

Slightly skeptical, Ranetta says, "Well...okay, if you say so." They jump out of the car as the movers are backing into the space next to them. What she didn't know was, Val's lying her ass off! There's no need for an audition to land a gig you're already famous for! Her quest was for that fifty, and the next stop, the dope man!

Bad Habits Revisited

Later that evening, a car honks, and Val walks to the window to see who it is; it's Calvin and his cousin, Rodney. She makes her way to the front door and yells out, "I'll see you later, Netta."

A voice from the back yells out, "Okay, be careful!" Val rushes out the door and locks it. She goes to the green Honda, jumps in, and they roll out. "So what's up, fellas?"

Calvin spoke first, "What's up, girl. This is my cousin, Rod."

Rodney says, "What's up?"

"I'm good…umm…Cal, were you able to connect with that dude you told me about?"

He says, "Yeah, babe, but you don't worry 'bout him right now. First thing's first, you gotta earn this money, honey!"

They arrive at Rodney's place, and he parks momentarily as he asks his cousin, "Yo, Cal…umm…you want me to go get that shit now or later?"

Calvin reaches into his pocket and pulls out a hundred-dollar bill, then hands it to him. "Here, I guess you can go get it now. She'll just have to owe me fifty, or she can hook you up later…you know…on me."

He gazes back at Val, who's sitting there with her arms crossed, a finger tapping and frowning. "So who the hell gave you the authority to make decisions for me, nigga?"

Calvin quips, "Well, excuse me! Do you want that shit or not? He's the one that knows the connect, not me!"

She just rolls her eyes and says, "Yeah, of course, I want it! But do you have to be such an asshole about it? Look, let me make my own decisions, you got it?"

"Yeah…I got it! If it's possible, dude, just give me twenty-five back, and you keep the rest for doin' this for me."

Rodney says, "Damn, chick, why you gotta be like that? Hell...I wanna have some fun, too!"

Val laughs, then says, "Fine, keep it like it was. Just make sure you bring me back that dime bag, and don't play me like I'm stupid, either!"

Rodney and Calvin look at each other and start laughing. Rodney, shaking his head, says, "Alright then...shit. I'll be back, cuz!" He gives his cousin some dap, then Calvin and Val get out of the car and disappear into the house as Rod takes off into the night.

A couple of hours later, he returns with what Val's been waiting for. Her and Calvin have long since finished their business as he walks in while they're watching television in the living room. Calvin asks, "Damn, dude...where the hell have you been? You get lost?"

"Naw, naw, cuz...just took a little longer than I'd thought it would, but...nonetheless, here you go, babe. I believe this belongs to you." He hands her the clear bag of white stuff.

"You damn right it does. I was getting worried! I hope this shit's worth it!" She has a razor blade and a few stirring straws laid out on the table in front of her. Val dumps a small pile of the cocaine on the table, then takes the razor and separates the powder into thin lines. Grabbing one of the straws, she bends down and inserts it in one of her nostrils, then holds down the other and sniffs up one of the lines. Sitting back up, she takes a couple of sniffs, shakes it off, and blurts, "Whoo...that's what I'm talkin' 'bout, baby!"

She bends down again and sniffs another line in the other nostril.

Smirking, Calvin slyly asks, "Damn...that good, huh? You don't mind if I try a couple of lines?"

She just shrugs, rubbing her nose and sniffing, and says, "Sure, why not."

He immediately jumps in and takes a couple of snorts. Now feeling the high kick in, she stands up and sort of wobbles a bit, then asks Rodney, "Hey, baby, you ready?"

He smiles and replies, "You damn skippy, I'm ready!" Excited, he stands and takes her by the hand, then yanks her to him. He reaches down and around to squeeze her butt.

She lets out a little squeal and starts giggling.

"Let's go to my room down the hall, ho!"

She stumbles, making her way down the hall, when *smack!* Rodney taps that butt. She lets out another little squeal. "You bad little boy!"

He replies, "Boy? Naw, baby, you ain't gonna think that when I get yo' ass in that room!"

Val disappears inside his room when he looks back at Calvin and says, "Thanks, cuz…whoo-wee! I'm gonna tear dat ass up, playa!"

Calvin just laughs and says, "Have fun, dawg!"

Rodney throws his thumbs up, sashays down the hall, enters his room, and closes the door behind him. Eventually, Calvin falls asleep on the couch watching TV. Better yet, it's watching him. Snoring, furiously, he's completely oblivious to the moans, groans, and screams coming from the back most of the night.

It's 1:05 a.m., and all of a sudden, *Bot! Bot! Bot! Bot! Blaow!* A woman screams in the distance as a car screeches off in the early morning darkness. The gunfire awakened everyone in the house. Calvin jumps up immediately and rushes to the front window. Rodney, half-naked, runs out of his room looking all crazy with a .38 in his hand. A fully naked Val followed, screaming out, "What the hell was that, Cal!"

Rodney says, "Damn, cuz…you see anything?"

"Hell no…scared the shit outta me, though! It sounded like it was right outside the door."

Val simply sighs then runs back in the room to get dressed.

"I know whatcha mean, cuz. It did sound close!" Calvin continues to peek out the window, then says, "Yo…I see this chick comin' out the house across the way on the phone. She looks like she's cryin'…whoa, dawg…"

Rodney interrupts, "What's up, cuz?"

"I think there's a body slumped over in that car. Damn…it looks like yours! Hell…it's the same color and everything. Anyway, it doesn't look too good, the window's busted out on the driver's side. I guess it's your standard drive-by. In the Dec, no doubt! At least that's something I've heard you say before, huh?"

Rodney, bewildered, replies, "What you talkin' 'bout, cuz? Drive-bys don't always happen in the Dec."

Calvin sighs a bit and shakes his head and says, "Naw, naw... I'm talkin' 'bout it's what you say all the time...you know, whenever somethin' goes down, you always have to end it with, 'In the Dec, no doubt.'" It dawns on him, then he laughs and says, "Oh...okay... yeah, yeah...you right!"

Fully dressed and ready to go, Val walks back into the living room. "Hey...could one of yaw take me home?"

Rodney turns and says, "Yeah...hold on, I'll go get a shirt and then we can be out."

By the time Rodney and Val walked out of the house, there were sirens and flashing lights in the near distance. Calvin was on the front lawn near the street, being nosy. Suddenly, several police cruisers pull up in both directions. The rescue pulls in just beyond the car the victim was in, as the police now quickly assess the damage. Some scout the area with flashlights in hand and guns drawn. One of the cops approaches the distraught woman and begins asking questions. Meanwhile, the paramedics rush to the shot man only to find he'd died instantly. They leave him there momentarily to allow the authorities to finish their investigation. "Excuse me...what's your name?"

"Marleena Crews," says the woman, still sobbing.

"What's your association to the victim?"

She sniffs and replies, "I was his girlfriend. He was off to work, and the next thing I know, he's shot up in his fuckin' car! Oh my god!" She breaks down as a female cop that's on the scene tries to comfort her as the male cop continues with his questioning.

"I'm sorry, ma'am...I just have to ask you a few more questions...umm...what's his name?"

She gathers herself a bit before answering, "Kerry Norton. He worked the graveyard shift at some warehouse on Moreland Avenue as a security guard." Still trying to maintain her composure, she continues, "Kerry ain't never, *never*, hurt nobody! He's always had many friends, no enemies that I know of. He was a very decent, hard-working man. I just can't believe somebody would just up and do him like that!"

The cop sympathizes with her, "I totally understand, ma'am. You said on the phone that there were two men in the car, right?"

"Yes…one was driving and the other one was…well, you know."

"Yes, I get it. So do you remember what kind of car it was?"

"Yeah, it was a black Crown Vic, with black rims and tinted windows…That's all I remember about it."

"That's a good start, Ms. Crews. Don't worry, we're gonna catch the monsters who did this, trust me!"

"I sure hope so," then she starts crying again.

As Rodney was driving Val home, he was thinking about the shooting. It weighed heavy on his mind because those shots were more than likely for him! The fact is, the so-called connect really is a dude he's been casing the last month and a half. Last night is when he finally decided to rob him. He held the dude up at gunpoint, snatched the kilo and five hundred dollars he had on him, and fled the scene, only to be pursued by the dude who picked up one of his homeboys on the way. He was able to shake them by dipping through a neighborhood not too far from where he lived. Laying low there for about thirty or so minutes, he then decided to creep home. Though it seemed sinister to be grateful that it was the other guy that got jacked and not him, he still felt a little pain for what happened. A single tear flowed down his cheek, then a gentle hand out of nowhere wiped it away. He jumped a bit and looked over at Val, who had a concerned look on her face. "What's wrong, Rod?"

"I feel bad 'bout dat dude back there. The whole situation's fucked up!"

She sighs and says, "Wow…yeah…all the times I've been out in the streets…I've never witnessed anyone actually getting murdered! I always see the aftermath. I mean, I don't ever wanna see any of it. You know, I don't mean to scare you, but I've shot someone and never seen the body drop. I was too chickenshit to see that, too chickenshit to walk into the room and do it, so I shot 'im through a wall."

With total shock, Rodney looks at her and exclaims, "Why the hell did you tell me that, shawty!"

She sits in silence for a moment then answers, "I don't know…I guess I'm just rambling. Hey, don't worry about it!"

"Naww...so who the hell was it?"

She smacks her lips and blurts, "I can't tell you that!"

"Damn, it's not like I know your ass, shawty! You can tell me!"

"No, I'm not sayin'. It's totally irrelevant now, anyway. It was a long time ago."

Rodney laughs a little and says, "You know what...I think you're bullshittin' me! You ain't shot nobody!"

She just shrugs and says, "Whatever...if you say so." He just kind of cuts his eyes at her for a minute, then silence the rest of the way.

Finally, Rodney pulls into the apartment complex and drives to Val's building. He parks, then turns to her and says, "Alright then, shawty. If it ain't a problem, can I see you tomorrow night? I got mo' of dat shit if you need it."

She smirks and answers, "I'll see...I've got your number. I'll give you a call." He shrugs and nods his head. She blows him a smooch, then exits the car and walks to her front door. Val turns and waves to him before disappearing inside. Rod backs out of the space and speeds off.

The Return

It's Saturday night at Club Boozy's. Ranetta and Val walk through the door at about ten o'clock. Looking the place over, Ranetta thinks to herself, *Wow, this is upscale, very plush indeed! A pretty water fountain greets the guests. The lighting and décor are on point…hmm…there has to be a woman behind all this. I know a man's not gonna be this particular.*

She looks over at Val and says, "Dang, you didn't tell me about all this! This place is *hot!*"

Val, with a confused look on her face, struggled to figure out what she was talking about. Then it dawns on her that she told Ranetta about an audition and meeting the owner. She quickly replies, "Oh…umm…I forgot! Yeah, the place is really nice." She plays it off nicely as Ranetta continued to look on in amazement. Calvin strolls in fifteen minutes later, walks up to this guy, and taps him on the shoulder, then asks, "What it is, Big Boozy?"

Floyd Clinton turns around in surprise, then blurts, "Oh…goddamn, man! It's been a long time…Calvin Kitchens! How ya doin'?" He extends his hand to shake Calvin's.

"So have you met Ranetta and Val yet?"

Floyd kind of looks around and says, "No…no, I haven't… ah…are they here?" That's when Calvin notices the ladies slowly but surely moving in their direction. "Yep, there they are right there."

Floyd peeps them out as they approached and says, "Ooo-kay… umm…not bad, my brotha…Is the older one single?"

Calvin kind of chuckles and answers, "Damn, you still a dirty ole dawg, huh?"

Floyd laughs and says, "Hey…you know how it is, Cal…Shit never changes much."

Calvin waves at the ladies as they walk up, then introduces them to Floyd. "Ranetta, Val, this is Floyd Clinton...you know, Big Boozy." He shakes their hands as he asks, "How you ladies doin'? So do you like the place?"

Ranetta answers first, "Oh, yes! Very nice, Mr. Clinton! I already know I'm gonna like workin' here."

Floyd gazes at her, smiles, and says, "Please call me Floyd, I insist. So what about you, darlin'? You feel the same way?"

Before Val could answer, Ranetta interrupts, "I thought you already met her?"

Floyd looks confused, as Val glared at Calvin, who spoke up fast, "Umm...we'll explain all that later, Netta...ah...right now you and my man here got some paperwork to go over."

Floyd kind of laughs to himself, then says, "Netta? Okay...I like that better. You don't mind if I call you that, do you?"

A little confused herself now, she replies, "Ah...yeah...no...ah, whatever...Mr. Clinton...I mean, Floyd, sorry!"

Laughing again, he says, "Hey, that's alright...umm...why don't you two follow me to my office." He nods his head toward some stairs that led up to the second floor. As the ladies follow, he glances back and says, "Hey, Cal...we'll rap later, alright?"

Calvin throws a hand up and replies, "No problem." He stands there, watching as they disappeared up the steps, beaming and thinking to himself, *Now it's finally time to put my plan into motion!*

Later on, after everything's squared away, Floyd tells the ladies to relax and enjoy the rest of the evening, not to mention, seizing the opportunity to get acquainted with Ranetta. They sit at one of the three immense bars and chat while Val mingles in the crowd. Floyd, smiling, asks, "So are you from Missouri originally?"

"No, I'm originally from Greenville, South Carolina. I went to Howard University and stayed in DC for about five years. I finally graduated and moved to St. Louis to take a job as a manager of a big department store. After ten long, grueling years in the retail business, I got totally burnt out, Whoo! Finally, I just took a chance and moved to New York on a humbug. That's where I got my first taste of working in a nightclub. The place was called Phoenix Wild, and

I worked there for about two years until I got a better offer from a place called the Flava Bar in lower Manhattan. I was able to hang in there for two years, but the cost of living in New York is murder! So I decided to move closer to my sister, Rosetta, who was living in Kansas City at the time. I stayed in Kansas City, Kansas, for about four years, back in retail, unfortunately. Couldn't take it anymore. I moved to Missouri and took a management position at a bank, where I worked for a year until taking ownership of a club my sister's husband used to own. This whole year has evolved into complete chaos…too much to even get into right now. I'd rather not talk about it, most of it is too painful. In fact, I've been runnin' my mouth too much! I know you're probably like, when is she gonna shut up?"

Floyd laughs and says, "No, no, no…I enjoy hearin' you talk. I want to get to know you better. If you want, you can continue."

She blushes and smiles, then says, "Nope, now I think it's your turn."

Smiling, he begins, "Well…I'm originally from Chicago…you know, that's where I met Calvin. He's from the same area. Anyway, I lived there until I was thirty-seven. I got into some trouble here and there, along the way. You know how it is when you're young and dumb?"

She shrugs and nods her head in agreement.

"I worked odd jobs to make ends meet, but I got tired of all that and decided to move to Jefferson City. I got a tip on a job there, but it really didn't pan out like I wanted it to, so it ended up being a brief stay, six months to be exact."

Ranetta remarks, "Wow, somewhere in there, we kinda crossed paths. I mean, we were almost in the same area!"

Chuckling, he replies, "Yep…that's true. Actually, very true because during that time, I would end up in Kansas City on occasions."

"So is that when you decided to move to Atlanta?"

Shaking his head, he answers, "No, actually, I went back to Chicago for a couple of years, then moved down here in the spring of 2004. From that point on, it's been one blessing after another!"

"Wow, that's awesome! I understand you have another business as well?"

"Oh, yes…it's a linen, uniform cleaning, and sales company. I'm in the process of expanding it. That's the main reason I was looking for someone to run this joint, so I can concentrate all my efforts on that business. I'm so glad we had this chat. Now I'm totally confident that you're exactly what I'm looking for."

Beaming, she says, "Oh, thanks! I'm gonna try my best not to let you down."

He smiles and says, "I'm definitely not worried about that."

Calvin walks up and interrupts, "So is everything set? Are y'all good?"

Floyd says, "Oh, yeah…it's a done deal." He chuckles and gives a wink in Ranetta's direction.

Calvin exclaims, "Outstanding…well, if you'd excuse me, I've got to take care of some business, so I'll see y'all later, okay?"

They both in unison say, "Okay." He strolls to the back heading for the restroom. Stopping momentarily at a table to pick up the plastic bag from the novelty shop that he stashed there earlier, then continues on.

The restroom was empty, but he had to be sure, so Calvin bent down to check both stalls. Satisfied that no one was there, he goes to the sink counter to drop the bag and locks the restroom door. He dumps all the contents from the bag and proceeds to spread out the six candles on the counter, then reaches over to retrieve the box of matches. Pulling one out, he strikes the side to light it, then lit each candle, one by one. After discarding the burnt match, he picks up Ben's old journal and flips through the pages until he finds the lines for the chant to erect Ben's old evil spirit once again! Calvin clears his throat then begins. Once he finishes, the flames on the candles rise and connect with one another. Standing there, stunned and wide-eyed, suddenly a flash occurs. The lights in the whole building go out for a few seconds, then they come back on except for the restroom. Calvin searches for the light switch in the darkness when…"What took you so long, nigga?" Sinister laughter followed for a few seconds before eventually fading. In a flash, the lights blinked back on as Calvin stood looking dumbfounded for a moment. He hesitates before asking, "Is that you, Ben?"

The voice bellows, "Who the hell else would it be, fool?"

Nervously, he laughs and says, "Of course, of course...ahh... they start work tomorrow night."

"Good! Good...then we start some shit tomorrow night! Have you found what you're lookin' for yet?"

"No...not yet, but I'm gonna get started soon, though."

The voice blurts, "Well, you better! Cuz ya see, when opportunity knocks for me, I'm gonna take it, literally!"

"Okay...okay, but I thought the plan was for me to get my hands on that money and—"

The voice angrily interrupts, "And? And, my ass! Remember, I'm in charge now. You better make it yo' business to find that loot, or else you'll be shit out of luck, partna!" Now the spirit disappears as Calvin blurts out, "Ben...hey, Ben? Shit!"

Pissed, Calvin gathers up the contraband and throws it all in the garbage can, then promptly leaves the restroom. As he storms out, he passes by the cleaning lady, who calls to him, "Excuse me, sir, is anybody else in there?"

"Naw...ain't nobody in there, lady!"

Shocked by his nasty attitude, she mumbles to herself before going into the restroom, "Damn, what the hell's buggin' him?"

He eventually spots Ranetta and walks up to her, then asks, "Hey, Netta, have you seen Val around?"

"No, so what was that all about earlier tonight? What you two got cookin' behind the scenes, huh?"

Shocked by the question, he addresses it by saying, "Cookin' behind the scenes...hell, ain't nothin' cookin'. I mean...sure we had a disagreement a while back, but it ain't no big deal now. Look...I'm just lookin' for her so we can set up some performances for the club, that's all!"

"Okay, so why are you concerned about that?"

"'Cuz I'm now in charge of coordinating all live performances...I thought you knew?"

"No, I didn't...Sorry! I haven't seen her in a minute."

"Well, if you do see her, please tell her to call me. I'd appreciate it, okay?"

"I will...oh, by the way, that power outage a minute ago gave me slight chills for some reason. I guess it's just bad memories. What about you?"

Half listening, Calvin replies, "Huh? Oh yeah...I guess briefly it did."

She stares at him crazily for a second, then asks, "Umm...you alright, Cal? You seem kinda out of it."

"Yeah...I'm cool," then starts walking off, saying, "Hey, I'll talk to you later...umm...Do you know where Floyd went?"

Still with a concerned look on her face, she says, "He went to his office to call the power company. Are you sure you're alright? You're acting rather peculiar all of a sudden."

He shoots her a glare and snaps, "Yes! I told you, I'm cool! I just need to talk to Floyd before I leave."

Throwing her hands up, she quickly replies, "Okay, I was just concerned...Take it easy!"

He stops short, exhales, and says in an even tone, "Sorry...you'll have to excuse me...I've got some shit on my mind I'm tryin' to deal with right now. Don't worry, though. I've got it under control." Then he quickly thinks to himself, *I hope.*

Ranetta just shrugs and says, "Okay, if you say so." He turns and walks away, leaving her there to look on, shaking her head.

Floyd's in his office on the phone when Calvin knocks on the half-closed door. He tells him to come in. As Calvin enters, he suddenly reaches behind him to close the door to the secret room that was directly behind his desk. Not quick enough, though, at least not before Calvin got a glimpse of what he's been looking for. The whole reason he came to Atlanta in the first place—it was the safe! It's in a private room next to Floyd's plush office. Smirking and thinking to himself, *Damn, that was easy!* Eventually, Floyd gets off the phone. "So what can I do for you, Cal?"

"Oh...nothin' much, man...umm...so you like Netta, huh?"

Floyd smiles, "Yeah, man. She's nice! I think she's gonna work out, and I like Val, too! She can sing, right?"

"Oh, yeah, dude. She's very talented, very!"

With a little nod, Floyd then says, "Hey, let's set something up for next weekend. I've got a band coming in to rehearse this week, so let's see if she can gel with them first, then we can have her debut on Saturday."

Smiling, Calvin says, "Sounds good to me." He extends his hand to Floyd, and they shake. "I'll let her know as soon as possible and then we can get to work on that, okay?"

"Cool...I'll holla at cha later, then." Calvin nods, turns, and just before he hops out of the office, "Oh...hey, dude, would you close the door on the way out? Thank you?"

"No problem, my brotha."

He walks out and closes the door, then takes a few steps, when *smack!* His head flies forward, and he immediately grabs the back of it and blurts, "Oww!"

In an even tone, the spirit says, "What's this next week bullshit, huh? I thought everything was goin' down tomorrow?"

Recovering, Calvin stands upright, collects himself, and says, "Look, that's what I was tryin' to tell you, earlier. This shit takes a little time to set up! You'll get your chance next week, partna!"

With a little more fury now, the spirit says, "Partna? I ain't cha damn partna, got it?" *Smack!* "This shit bettah happen next week or else!"

Now the spirit vanishes, leaving Calvin rubbing his head again. He looks around to see if anyone saw what just happened. Fortunately, no one did, so he just shakes it off and strolls out of the club, whistling. He's happy for a week because this gives him time to plan when and how he'll break into that safe and snatch that loot!

Still Running Wild

It's Saturday morning, and Ranetta's a little frantic because Val never made it home. She's called her phone several times. No answer. She decides to call Calvin. "Hello?"

"Yes, how you doin', Calvin? Have you heard from or seen Val? I've been callin' and callin', but she doesn't answer!"

"Hold on a minute, Netta." He cuffs the receiver and turns toward Val. *Slurp! Slurp! Slurp!* He whispers, "Hey! Hey, you!" That's when Rodney taps Val on the head. *Slurp! Smack!*

She whirls around and yells, "What? Can't you see I'm in the middle of something!"

Calvin answers, "I can see that. You got yo' phone on, girl? Netta's been tryin' to reach you. She's worried about you, chick!"

"Damn, I lost it! Umm...just tell her I'm alright. Make something up. I don't care!" She goes right back to what she was doing, but with more intensity. Rodney starts grunting and shifting in his seat with his hand on top of her head. Calvin gets up and walks into the other room just in time, as Rodney pops his load! "Hey...umm...she just walked in from outside. She was out there talkin' to my cousin and just told me she lost her phone."

"Well...can I talk to her?" He hears the bathroom door close in the background and answers, "Damn, she just went into the bathroom. Do you want me to tell her to call you when she comes out?"

"Duh...of course! I've been worried about her. So what, does she have a thing for your cousin or something?"

"Umm...you can say that."

"Wow, she could've at least given me a heads-up. I mean—"

She's interrupted by immediate laughter. "So what the hell's so funny?"

"Oh, nothing...don't mind me. I'm just bein' silly right now."

"Yeah...and if you'd ask me, both of you've been kinda silly lately! Look...just tell her now that I know where she is, to call me later. I've got some errands to run. She can call me on my cell, okay?"

"Okay, will do."

She hangs up, and he starts laughing again, saying to himself, "Heads-up...that's a good one!"

It's 5:35 p.m., and Val meets Ranetta at a place called Rocky's Pizzeria, downtown. She walks up to Ranetta and gives her a hug. "Hey, sorry I didn't call you sooner. I think I laid my phone down at the club, and well, you know how that goes."

Ranetta just waves her hand. "Don't worry about it. As long as you're safe and sound, that's all I care about. You can order what you want. I've got to go to the ladies' room first."

"Okay...but I'm treatin'."

"What? You treatin'? You don't have the money to do that now, do you?"

"Yes, I do. I can pay for it! What do you want?"

Ranetta shrugs, "Okay...well, I'd like two slices of pepperoni with extra cheese and a Sprite, thanks."

"No problem." The waiter comes and she puts in the order.

They finish their early dinner and head home. On the way, Ranetta decided to stop by the mall first to pick something up to wear to the club. Val stays in the car while she ran in real quick. Spotting Ranetta's phone, she reaches for it and calls Rodney. "Hey, baby, can we party tonight?"

"Damn, baby...umm...shit! I ain't got no loot fo' you tonight! I got to get through the week, but I do got dat shit for you doe, shawty."

"That's cool...I mean, that's what I'm talkin' 'bout, anyway."

"Cool...when you want me to pick you up?"

"Tonight, at the same club you picked me up last night. I'll call you later."

"Bet...I got to pick up some more rubbers, anyway."

"Alright then...bye."

"Later, shawty."

Later on that evening, while en route to the club, Rodney stops by a convenience store. He parks his car, then gets out and is slightly distracted by a couple in the car next to his arguing loudly. He moves on, laughing to himself, as he walks into the store mumbling, "In the Dec…no doubt." Rodney goes straight to the beer cooler to cop a six-pack. He chooses his soldiers of choice, then suddenly gets the munchies and strolls down one of the aisles. Gazing at the various snacks, he happens to look up and notice the cat in the other aisle. It was the homeboy he snatched the kilo from. The dude's running his mouth on the phone, completely oblivious to Rodney's presence. So he quickly looks back down to the snacks and grabs a bag of chips and rushes to the counter. He asks for a pack of condoms and a box of squares. As the clerk was ringing him up, he quickly glances back at the dude. Their eyes meet, looking at each other for a second or two. Rodney's interrupted by the clerk, who gives him his total. He turns and pays while the dude abruptly ends his call, then just stands there, pondering. Rodney grabs the bag from the clerk and without looking in the dude's direction, rushes toward the entrance. He gets to the door when it finally clicks in the dude's head.

"Dammnn, you the—"

Now Rodney makes a mad dash to his car!

"Hey, you! I thought dat was yo' ass!"

He rushes for the door. Rodney starts his car up, then backs out as the dude steps outside the door screaming, "Goddammit…I'm gonna get you, muthafucka!"

Rodney speeds off. The dude turns around and finds himself staring down the barrel of a twelve-gauge shotgun! "Goddamn! What the fuck, man? What's wrong with you?"

The clerk screams, "You not pay! You not pay, muthafuckah!"

The dude looks down and now realizes he had a cold forty in his hand. He was about to get dropped over a damn two-dollar bottle of malt liquor! He eases back into the store slowly. "Okay, okay, take it easy. I'm gonna pay for it, dawg."

The clerk screams, "I'm not cho dawg, homey! I tired of you scum comin' in store stealin'!"

He nervously laughs, as he's paying, "Scum? Man…I come in here all the fuckin' time. Yo…and I pay all the time, too! I guess I won't be comin' back, that's fo' sho'!"

The clerk puts the gun down behind the counter and gives the dude his change and a bag, then says, "Good…you leave now," then points toward the door as a woman standing outside nervously peers into the store. The dude just shakes his head, puts the forty in the paper bag, and bounces.

Val's waiting outside Club Boozy's when Rodney pulls up. She jumps in, and they speed off. "Hey, baby, you sounded kind of paranoid when I talked to you on the phone a few minutes ago. You alright?"

He just shakes his head and continues to drive in silence. Eventually, she speaks up and asks, "So you not talkin' tonight?"

He turns to her. "How do you feel about a change of scenery? Like a hotel or something?"

Val, surprised, asks, "Damn…I thought you had to get through the week? How're you gonna spring for a room? You know I can't right now."

"I know, I know…I just realized that I had a little something extra, and besides, I don't feel like goin' all the way back to my crib."

Little did she know he was too damn scared to go back to his place right now. He knew Calvin would be alright, and it's not like the dude actually knew where he lived, but who's to say him and his homeboy won't cruise the neighborhood just to see what was up. Rodney wasn't taking any chances, so he rolls up to a Motel 6 and parlays there for the rest of the night.

Meanwhile, at the club, Rudy "Li'l Rude" Taylor strolls in and is greeted with a handshake and a hug from Floyd.

"How's my favorite cousin doin'? Are you ready to rock the house tomorrow? Tickets have been sellin' fast, baby! You're truly one of the hottest comedians around!"

Rudy beams, "Aww…I'm totally flattered! Wow, I am indeed. I mean, being yo' favorite cousin and all. All that other shit…well, I already knew."

Floyd starts laughing, "See, negro, there you go!"

They both laugh as Rudy says, "Naww...you know I'm just playin'! I feel truly blessed, cuz. It's fun travelin' around the country makin' people laugh and then to get paid for it! It's definitely a blessing."

"Yeah, I hear ya, cuz. Oh yeah...I want you to meet someone." Floyd urges his cousin to follow him to one of the bars. Ranetta was chatting with the bartender as Floyd attempted to introduce her, "Hey, Netta, I want you to meet my cousin."

"Oh, hey...Li'l Rude, isn't this a small world?" Both men look at each other, shocked, then start laughing. "Damn...you know me? I don't think I know you, but you do look a little familiar."

"Yeah, you performed at the Wall back in Missouri."

Rudy's eyes widened, "Ohh, dammnn...you talkin' 'bout that place that mysteriously burned to the ground ten minutes after I'd left? Man...if it wasn't for me chasin' some chick, I'd have been still there! Wow! So were you in the crowd, worked there, or what?"

She kind of hesitates, then looks at Floyd, who had a curious look on his face and answers, "Well, I was the owner."

Both men are stunned as Floyd says, "Wow, so that's what you meant when you said this whole year has evolved into complete chaos. Umm...what happened?"

"Well, the report from the arson detective stated it was a faulty electrical system. There were *no* signs of arson, anywhere!"

He puts a finger up and quickly says, "Hey, I'm not accusing you of anything. I'm just curious, that's all."

She shakes her head in agreement. "I know, I know...I just wanted to make that crystal clear! I don't want you to lose faith in me."

Shaking his head, Floyd says, "No, no, don't worry about that! Hey, shit happens."

Rudy's confused now, "Umm...crystal clear? Why does she have to make anything clear? I don't understand."

Floyd quickly explains, "Oh...she's my new manager."

Rudy gives a crazy look like, "Are you sure about that, boss?" Then busts out laughing as Ranetta and Floyd shake their heads in disgust. "That's not funny!" Floyd agrees, and Rudy stops laughing and says, "I know…I'm sorry! I'm stupid…Don't mind me." Floyd and Ranetta look at each other, then start chuckling and in unison blurt, "Umm-hmm!"

She extends her hand to Rudy, he chuckles and shakes her hand. "Hey, welcome to Club Boozy's."

"Thanks."

They all go to Floyd's office now to chat and reminisce. Naturally, Ranetta couldn't tell Floyd or Rudy the truth about what really happened. They wouldn't understand at all. As they're walking toward the office, they don't notice Calvin peering down at them from one of the control booths behind the VIP section. He smirks, concentrating most of his attention on Rudy.

A Matter of Sixty G's

Calvin sits behind a control board figuring out all the features. Being the talent coordinator, he needed to know how to work the lighting effects, sound, etc. Soon, he decides that he wants a drink, so he calls down to one of the bars to order one. Minutes later, an attractive waitress shows up with his drink in tow. She hands it to Calvin. He thanks her and slides her a tip. Flashing that pretty smile, she thanks him, winks, and as she starts to head back toward the stairs. Out of nowhere, Rudy strolls around the corner and almost bumps into her. "Whoa…damn…hello there, beautiful!"

The waitress laughs. "Oh…hello, Rudy!"

Calvin exclaims, "Heyyy…what's up, man? Do you remember me?"

Distracted from Ms. Foxy, who quietly slips away and disappears down the stairs. "Ahh…no dude, can't say that I do."

"Yeah…I introduced you on stage when you came to the Wall in Missouri. You remember…the talent showcase? I was the MC and prop manager there."

Rudy lifts his brows, "Oh, okay…now I remember. Damn, Netta was right. This is a small world! So what's up, my brotha?"

Rudy gives him some dap. "Nothin' much, man…you know, just kickin' it. Your cousin and me go way back."

"Yeah, I remember you telling me something like that. Hell, I was so drunk then, I'm surprised I remember anything."

They both laugh at his statement, then Calvin says, "Yeahhh… you were feeling no pain that night. In fact, I remember you telling me that you were gonna unite with your cousin and expand the business with the cheddar he's got stashed away somewhere."

Rudy just kind of smirks, "Well, actually that ain't happenin'. I mean, between us, he acquired somewhat of a gambling problem, and well, I don't think he's got much stashed away anymore. I know he's still got quite a bit, but not enough to do that. Anyhow...shit, I'm too busy now! You know he's still gonna expand that other business. That's why he hired Netta to run the joint so he can concentrate all his efforts on that."

Calvin cracks a smile. "Well, hell...it's all good then!" Though in the back of his mind, he's pissed!

Rudy smiles. "And you know it! Hey, brah...ahh...don't mean to cut you off or nothin', but that chick...wooo-woo, got tah go holla, ya know?"

Calvin kind of chuckles and says, "Yep, I gotcha, playa!"

Rudy gives him some dap and yells out, "Peace!" then disappears around the corner and down the stairs. Suddenly from behind, Ben's voice exclaims, "Well, well, well...not exactly what you thought, huh?"

Shaking his head, Calvin says, "No, not exactly, but no matter what, I'm breakin' into that safe! I'm gonna get whatever I can get. Believe that shit, Ben!"

"You better do whatever you gonna do this week because by the weekend, I'm takin' dat bitch back to hell with me...as well as Big Boozy! I see that the simple-minded son of a bitch is still up to his old tricks."

"Yeah, no doubt! Yo, it's goin' down this week, don't you worry."

"Oh, I'm not worried about shit! You the one that needs to be worried."

"So what the hell's that supposed to mean?"

There's nothing but complete silence as Calvin nervously sat. "Hello? Hello...are you there?" Still not a sound. "Damn it!" He punches his hand in anger.

Meanwhile, at the motel, Rodney and Val have finished taking care of their business and are laid up in bed watching TV. They eventually finish off the chips he'd bought earlier, but they were still hungry. He decides to run across the street to the gas station for more snacks. As he walks across the road, he stops short. At the far end of the lot was a black Crown Vic with black rims and tinted windows. He stands there watching as the driver gets out of the car and strolls into the store chatting on his phone. Rodney decides to duck behind the building and run to the other side. He peeks around the corner and spots the car. He waits until the dude comes back out, jumps into his ride, and jets out of the parking lot before he enters the store. Rodney quickly goes in and gets whatever he's going to get and leaves without hesitation.

The next day, Rodney is posted up in his usual hustling spot, shaking off the rest of the dope he had when it suddenly dawns on him that he didn't stash any away for Val. *Welp, there goes that piece of pussy!* he thinks to himself while reaching for his phone, calling her only to get his suspicion fulfilled. "Heyyy, what it is, shawdy? We hookin' up later?"

"You got what I like, baby?"

With slight hesitation, "Umm...no, not tonight. My connect is outta town, and I don't know when he'll be back, but...umm...I got some money though."

"Actually...I got other plans now that I think about it."

"Awlright then."

She hangs up without even saying goodbye.

"Just like I fuckin' thought!" Slapping his phone back into the belt clip, he jumps into his car and dips through the Dec, trying to see if he could hook up with one of his other chicks.

Val calls the dude that slipped her his number while she was waiting on Rodney at the club the other night. The phone rings. A guy answers, "Hello?"

"Hey...is this Paul?"

"Yeah...who's this?"

"My name's Valencia. You gave me your number outside of Club Boozy's. I remember you sayin' that you knew where to go to get fucked up. What I want to know is, do they have plenty of that white snow around?"

Chuckling. "Hell yeah, shawdy! Anything you want, shawdy!"

"Cool...what time can you pick me up?"

"Whenever. Where you at?"

Two hours later, Paul pulls up in an Expedition sitting on twenty-fours, bumping some of that old school West Coast shit! She jumps in. He scopes her up and down, smiling with a blunt at the corner of his mouth, and they roll out. It's obvious now that Val has totally slipped back into the sanctums of complete devilment. Reverting to her old ways, Val's focus has drifted away from school and even her singing. Unfortunately, Ranetta's focus has kind of drifted away from her as well. She didn't even question where Val was going because she was preoccupied with deciding what to wear for a trip to the mountains with Floyd. The two seem to have hit it off pretty fast. Floyd was picking her up that early evening and driving up to Rock City in the Georgia mountains. They're going to spend the rest of the day sightseeing, then drive over to Chattanooga and spend the night at a hotel. Floyd pulls up in a black Escalade and honks the horn. Ranetta appears with her overnight bag in tow. When she reaches the SUV, he greets her, grabs the bag, and places it in the back with his. They both jump in and begin making their way to I-75 north. Ranetta gets a call from Val as they're rolling up the highway.

"What's up, girl? Sorry I didn't get a chance to talk to you before you left."

"Oh, that's alright. I'm with a friend I met at the club, so don't wait up. I might be getting in late."

"Hey, that's cool. I won't be home anyway. I'm on my way to the mountains now with a friend. We'll be back tomorrow afternoon or evening."

Shocked, Val says, "What? Who? Male or female?"

Ranetta smacks her lips and blurts, "Look at you, Ms. Nosy... Why?"

Val starts laughing, "Oooh, Auntie! Uumm, ummm, ump!"

Giggling, Ranetta says, "You need to stop! I'll talk to you later."

Continuing to tease, she replies, "Umm-hmmm...no doubt! I want all the naughty details, too!"

"Whatever. Bye!"

Val snickers, "Bye," then they both hang up. Now it seems that Calvin has the opportunity he's been waiting on. Once he got wind of them going out of town, he gathered up some of the necessary tools to do the job.

It's 6:05 p.m., Sunday evening, and Calvin unlocks the door at the side entrance of the club. He walks in carrying a bag filled with a flashlight, crowbar, hammer, screwdriver, and a nine-millimeter handgun. He turns toward the keypad on the wall to disarm the alarm system. After punching in the code, he reaches into the bag to grab the flashlight when the light in the hallway mysteriously comes on. He nearly jumps out of his shoes!

Ben's voice suddenly bellows, "You don't need that! I guess I can understand the crowbar, hammer, and screwdriver and even the damn flashlight, but why the fuckin' gun? Ain't nobody here, fool!"

Calvin collects himself and says, "I'm gonna make it look like somebody broke in the joint. The gun's for my protection."

The voice laughs. "Umm, umm, ump! You're not the brightest brotha, are you? I've sat back and waited and waited for you to ask for my help in all this...you know, so you wouldn't have to make a mess of all this shit, but no, look at you!"

"Now hold on. I didn't know you were willing to help! Furthermore, how the hell you gonna crack dat safe?"

"Do you see me, clown?"

"Hell no I can't see you. What kind of a question is that?"

"Precisely, fool! I was present on many occasions when that bastard opened the safe. I know the combination." Now very agitated, Calvin screams, "So why the fuck didn't you tell me that a while back, Ben?"

"Cuz you didn't ask, muthafucka. Calm yo' ass down! We need to take care of this business now!"

So without further incident, they make their way to Floyd's office. Once there, Calvin says, "I don't have a key to his office."

The voice responds, "No problem." Suddenly there's a pop sound, and the doorknobs fall off on both sides of the door. Calvin pushes it and enters as the light comes on. He notices the same thing happening to the other door leading into the mystery room where the safe is.

"Damn! I see whatcha mean now...nice, neat, and easy!"

"Told ya. The combination is 36-23-39...got it?"

"Yeah, got it." He walks over to the safe, drops the bag, and unzips it. He reaches back up to the dial and turns it clockwise a couple of times, then puts in the combination. He pulls up the handle and *click*, it opens! Smirking fiercely, he peers inside and starts to pull out the neat stacks of money wrapped in rubber bands. "Now we talkin'...woo-wee!"

"You just remember...in fact, I want my revenge this week. When she's rehearsing with the band, you got it?"

He stops momentarily, "Hey, that's no problem, but what about Boozy? I don't think he's gonna be in this week."

"Don't worry about that asshole. I'll get him when I get him. You just make sure that bitch shows up!"

Calvin shakes his head up and down nervously, then goes back to stuffing his bag with money. Once he's finished and leaves the room, the light goes out. They continue to go off behind him as he makes his way back to the side entrance. He resets the alarm, hurries out, and locks the door. The alarm sets, and the lights in the hallway go out. He jumps into an old pickup truck he got from one of his cousin's friends for $1,200 and rolls out. As he's heading down the street, a black stretch limo passes by and eventually turns into the parking lot of Club Boozy's.

It's 6:36 p.m., and Rudy exits the limo, running his mouth to some chick as usual. He makes his way to the front entrance. On the inside now, he disarms the security system and turns on the lights. He continues rambling, "Awww, damn, baby...why it gotta be like dat? Come on now...just come down to the club. I'll make sure you get VIP passes for you and yo' friends. Okay, darlin'? I got you!"

Rudy finally makes his way back toward Floyd's office. "So are you comin' or what? Cool...Doors open at eight. I'll see ya, bye." He puts his phone in his pocket, pulls out his keys in an attempt to unlock the door, and stops short. "What the fuck!"

Looking down, he spots the doorknob on the floor. Rudy reaches down and picks it up, completely dazed. He pushes the door open and finds the light switch. *Click*. He slowly walks in, looking around, and stops short again. "What the hell is goin' on here!" The other door was still open, and the doorknob was on the floor. He places the one he had in his hand on Floyd's desk and enters the room. After turning on the light, he immediately gazes around the room, checking for anything else out of place. The fancy full bar seem still intact, as well as all the pillows on the plush couch and love seat in the middle. The safe on the wall is closed, but... *Wait a damn minute! Safe? Sooo this is where it is*! he thinks to himself. He walks up to it and lifts the handle. It opens!

"Whaaat?" He quickly looks inside...empty! Baffled, he pulls out his phone and calls Floyd.

"What it is, cuz? You getting ready for tonight?" Ranetta giggles in the background and whispers to Floyd, "Tell him I said hello."

"Hey, Netta says what's up."

"Yeah...ahhh...tell her I said hello, but, cuz—"

Floyd interrupts, "Yo...is everything cool, cuz?"

"Well, actually no! I think the club's been hit."

"What! Whatcha mean the club's been hit? I ain't got time for no damn silly jokes right now, Rudy! I'm up here havin' a good ole time with my new friend! You need to stop playin'!" Floyd starts laughing as Rudy clears his throat and says, "Welp...umm...I'm not jokin', Big B...umm...somethin' seriously isn't right."

There's silence for a second or two before Floyd says, "Huh... hold on a minute." He excuses himself away from Ranetta and walks outside the room. "Okay, talk to me from the beginning."

"Okay...well, Fred brought me to the club. I came in, turned off the alarm system, and turned on all the lights as usual. I went directly to your office to get that package you wanted me to give to Mick and his crew for settin' up the place. By the way, it's here untouched. Anyway, I pulled out my keys to unlock the door and found that the doorknobs were on the damn floor!"

"What! On the floor?"

"Yeah...on the floor! Anyhow, I walk in to turn on the lights and noticed the same thing happened with the other door..."

Floyd immediately blasts, "Nooo...not that one too! What did they take?" In the back of his mind, he was hoping that it was not the safe that was hit, but he had a sinking feeling it was.

"All that I can tell you is that the safe was open."

Floyd explodes, "Oh, shit! Please don't tell me that! Did they pop the lock? What?"

"Please calm down, cuz. No, they didn't pop the lock. It was just open, like someone knew the combination."

"Open? That can't be right. I'm the only one that knows the combination, Rude!"

"Hey…I'm tellin' you, cuz, When I went in that room lookin' around, there was nothing else out of place! Nothing else broken or knocked over…nothin'! I walked over to the safe, lifted the handle, and *boom*, it was unlocked!"

Floyd blasts, "Shit! All my personal stash, gone! Sixty g's, Rude! Sixty damn g's!"

Rudy sympathizes with his cousin, "Wow, cuz…oh my, my… damn! I'm so sorry to hear that! So what can I do? Do you want me to call the police?"

Trying to get a grip of himself, Floyd mutters, "Yeah…yeah… umm…I guess…to have it on record, anyway. It's not like we can do any fuckin' thing about it now! Who the hell would do this to me? It's probably an inside job, but then again, maybe not. I don't know…So fuckin' confused right now! All I do know, Rude, is that I've been fucked with no Vaseline!"

In the distance, unnoticed by Rudy, there's a low, sinister laugh brewing, then it slowly dissipates.

Now What?

It's 7:30 p.m., and in thirty minutes, the club will open. Rudy finishes up with the police, and just before they leave, one of the officers asks, "Mr. Taylor, why doesn't Mr. Clinton have a surveillance camera in his office?"

"Hell, according to him, he felt there wasn't a need since no one was supposed to know about that safe in the secret room. The club's money is kept in a safe in the back office just beyond the kitchen. That's where all the cameras are, as well as the three bars."

"I understand, Mr. Taylor. We've got this list and your statement, so we'll be in touch."

Looking confused, Rudy says, "Be in touch? Why? It's not my money!"

"We understand that, Mr. Taylor, but everyone on this list who knows the code to disarming the system is a suspect."

"Damn...I'm the one dat called y'all!"

"Yep, like I said, we'll be in touch."

As the officers leave the club, he stands there looking dumbfounded, thinking, *How can I be a damn suspect when I didn't do a damn thing!*

The new assistant manager, Byron Willows, walks in and greets Rudy. "Yooo! Li'l Rude's in dah house! So you 'bout tah do ya thang shortly, huh?" He attempts to give Rudy a high five, but he's still lost in thought, completely oblivious to anything he just said. "Yo...you there, Rude?" He waves his hand in front of his face.

Snapping back to reality, Rudy replies, "Oh...Oh!...yeah, what's up, Bee?"

"So what's wrong, man? You seem out of it."

Sighing, he answers, "Dude, the club was hit today! Somebody swiped some money out of Big Boozy's office!"

Shocked, Byron says, "Oh…that's why those cops were here! Have you called your cousin about it?"

"Hell yeah, that's who I called first! You know the whole fucked-up situation is that they said I'm a goddamn suspect. Me! I'm the one dat called them!"

"Wow, are you serious? What makes them suspicious of you?"

He shrugs and answers, "Because I'm one of a few that knows the code to the security system. See, you should be glad you're just startin' tonight and my cousin didn't get a chance to give it to you yet, or else you'd be on the damn list too. He asked me to tell you the code when you got here."

Byron frowns and crosses his arms and says, "Hold on, do you mean to tell me somebody disarmed the system, came in and robbed the place, then rearmed it and left?"

Rudy shakes his head in major disgust and blurts, "Apparently. It was armed when I got here!"

"So who else knows the code?"

"Well…me, of course, my cousin and Ranetta, but they're out of town, as you know. Ummm…Big Herb, chief of security, who showed up five minutes after I did. The police questioned him already, though. Then there's the chef, Susan, who's not here tonight! Then finally, Calvin Kitchen, the talent coordinator, who is supposed to be here by now! Hold on…I need to call him. Excuse me."

"Oh sure. Hell, I've got to get things set up anyway." Byron walks off as Rudy dials up Calvin's number. After a few rings, he picks up, "Hello?"

"Hey, dude, where you at?"

"Who's this?"

"It's me, Rudy!"

"Oh…Li'l Rude, what's up? I'm turnin' in the parking lot now."

Rudy quips, "Good! Cuz, mannn, we've got a serious problem!"

"What kind of problem?"

"I'll tell you all about it when you get in here."

Calvin parks his truck, hops out, and bops up to the entrance, whistling. He's, of course, on top of the world because of accomplishing his goal, the sixty grand stashed in a safe place. He sees Rudy and walks over. "Sooo what's goin' down?"

Slowly shaking his hand, Rudy begins to explain, "Somebody broke into the joint and made off with a lot of money. It's definitely an inside job, I know. Whoever it was knows the code to disarm the system."

Playing like he's shocked, Calvin says, "Damn...are you serious?"

Shaking his head, Rudy continues, "Ummm-hmmm...and I hate to be the bearer of bad news, but everyone who knows the code is a suspect." He just kind of looks at Calvin, trying to notice any body language that will give him away.

Calvin coolly smirks and shrugs, "I'm not worried about that because I've got nothin' to hide and I've got a sound alibi."

Pausing for a moment and seeing no signs, Rudy says, "Well... that's good. Glad to hear it. Most of us seem to have one, but unfortunately, we'll have to wait until the investigation is over before we're all cleared."

Calvin says, "Well, you know how it is with the police and their investigations. They have to find concrete evidence to make their move or let it go. I wouldn't worry about it, dude. You know you're innocent, I know I am, and I don't know about anyone else. Hell, they'll probably figure it out sooner or later."

"Yeah...but it's still all fucked up! I don't want to be a suspect to anything!"

"Hey, I'm sure your cousin's got insurance. I think he'll be alright."

"No, Cal, insurance ain't gonna cover it! This wasn't the club's money. It was cuz's personal stash! Sixty g's, to be exact!"

Putting on like he's shocked, Calvin says, "Damn...whoa! That's a lot of money!"

"Yep, exactly!"

Calvin thinks, *Wow...so that's how much it is! Well, well, well, that's not a bad lick after all! Cool!*

Nine o'clock rolls around, and Rudy takes the stage. Considering all that has happened, he handles it like a pro and gives a good performance. When he was done, though, his mind drifted right back to the situation. Usually, he points to the crowd, pumps his fist, and beats on his chest a couple of times as the crowd roars with cheers and applause. Tonight, Rudy just smirks, waves one time, and kind of tosses the microphone to Calvin as he leaves the stage.

Calvin immediately jumps into MC mode, "Alright! Alright! Y'all give it up for Li'l Rude!"

The claps and cheers get louder with some whistling here and there as Rudy continues toward the back, oblivious to all the accolades.

It's Monday evening, Floyd drops Ranetta off at her apartment. He offers to take her bag in, but she insists on taking it in herself. He gives her a kiss, and she gets out of the SUV and retrieves the bag from the back compartment. She approaches the front door, sets the bag down, and turns to wave back at Floyd. He honks the horn, backs out, and speeds off, heading straight for the club, no doubt, to see the damage for himself.

Ranetta drops her bag and immediately checks her messages. The first one: "Hello…umm…you don't know me, but my name's Mable Thomas. I really hate to bring bad news, but…I found Valencia, your niece, left out on a curb in East Atlanta. She was gang-raped and beaten up pretty bad. I rushed her to Grady, and that's where you'll find her. Like I said, I'm so sorry you have to hear all this! My number is—" The answering machine cuts her off.

Ranetta just stands there, petrified!

The second message: "Hello, this is Mable again. I was cut off! If you didn't get the number, it's 679-781-3729. Please call me as soon as you get this message. Thank you."

The third message: "Hello, Netta? Hey, I'm at Grady Memorial. It's downtown. That's all I know. Please come when you can?"

She just flops on her couch and starts to cry. Now she starts to think, *Damn! First, Floyd gets robbed! Now I find out something even worse has happened! Oh my god, why?* She weeps for a moment, then reaches for the phone. Taking a long breath, she dials Mable's number, and soon she answers, "Hello?"

"Hi, Ms. Thomas…this is Ranetta Gibbs. I'm calling about Valencia…umm…Where's the hospital located?"

Then she breaks down. "Oh my god, chile! I'm so glad you called me! I can meet you somewhere, and we can go in my car together."

Ranetta gathers herself and says, "Thank you…thank you for everything! You are a godsend!"

"Honey, it's no problem at all! I'm so tired of what our beautiful, young sistas are goin' through out here! It's pitiful! Where do you live?"

"I live at 1207 Paramount Drive, and the apartments are called Westpark Estates. We're located in Fulton County."

"Okay, do you know where the capital building is downtown?"

Still sobbing, she sniffs and answers, "No, we just moved here last week."

Mable sighs and says, "You know what, I'll just come and pick you up."

Suddenly, Ranetta remembers, "Oh, hold on, I have a navigation system in my car! I'll find it!"

"Are you sure?"

"Yes, Grady Memorial Hospital, right?"

"Right. I'll meet you there."

Ranetta perks up a bit and replies, "Alright, I'm on my way out the door now!" She hangs up the phone, grabs her purse and keys, then races out the door.

Later on that evening in Val's hospital room, Ranetta's trying to make sense of what happened. "Who were these guys, Val?"

"I don't know any of them…except Paul, and I really don't know him that well. One minute, I'm at the party havin' fun, then we go to a hotel room to continue the party. Next thing I know, they all come in and jump me, and I eventually black out."

Ranetta and Mable sit in horror as she continues, "When I came to, we were in somebody's car. I started to speak, and this dude just slapped me, then told me to shut up! That's when the car stopped suddenly, and a guy on the front passenger side gets out and opens the back door. He yanks me out, and I scream, then he just tosses me aside like I was a piece of trash! He gets back into the car, and it speeds off. I hit the ground and couldn't move. I just froze up. I felt like I was gonna die!"

Ranetta starts weeping and says, "Oh my god!" over and over.

Mable blasted, "*Damn animals!* I swear, some men are nothin' but vicious animals! They need to be snatched up and have their weenies cut off! Maybe then they won't have the urge to brutalize another woman again!"

Meanwhile, Floyd's still at the club assessing the damage. He's called over Big Herb Wilcox to get more clarity on the situation. "Herb…I mean, *what the fuck!* There are cameras at the entrance and, of course, around the bars. They had to have captured something!"

Herb shakes his head. "Naw, boss. Nothing! If you want to see the tapes for yourself…in fact, yeah, let's go check 'em out right now. Maybe you can catch something I didn't see."

They both walk to the security booth, and Herb taps on the computer's keyboard, then brings up the footage in question. As they're viewing it, Floyd suddenly says, "There, did you see that?"

Bewildered, Herb asks, "What? I didn't see anything!"

"Okay, go back."

He does that, then as the image plays, Floyd says, "Stop there!" He quickly pauses it. "Alright, now look at the time. It says 6:03 p.m. Now continue to play it."

Herb starts the video again. Suddenly the time jumps to 6:38 p.m. He exclaims, "Damn! See…that's why I wanted you to see this shit for yourself! I didn't notice that before!"

Floyd rubs his chin as he says, "So that means somebody turned off the cameras for thirty-five minutes, but I don't see how that's possible. The cameras can only be turned off here! Look, there's Rudy right there turning on the lights!"

"Well, more than likely, there had to be two of them at work. One was already inside, somehow, and another came in and dismantled all the locks on the doors. Of course, I don't get that part though."

"Umm-hmm…I think you're right, Herb. I mean, I can see one of them turnin' back on the system and leavin' without being detected, but what about the other one? Unless there's a way to set a timer or something for the cameras to come back on."

Herb, shaking his head, says, "No, your system is not that sophisticated. It's like you said…everything has to be programmed from here manually."

Floyd's phone rings, "Hello…oh, hey, Netta. What's up?"

"It's a long story."

"Wow, you sound kinda down in the dumps right now!"

"Yeah, something bad has happened."

"Aw, hell…Now what?"

The Grim Reaper's Hot Rod

It's Tuesday afternoon. Calvin decides to call Val up and see if she could come over to the club and rehearse with the new band. The phone just rings and rings. He hangs up and calls Ranetta. "Hello?"

"Hey, Netta, is Val around? I wanted to know if she was available to rehearse with the new band today at the club."

"Oh, wow...so you haven't heard! She's in the hospital... umm...don't want to go into detail right now...Ah, it's too personal. Let's just say, she won't be singin' no time soon."

"What? Damn...what the hell happened, Netta?"

Ranetta sighs. "It's like I said, Calvin. It's too personal!"

"Wow, alright...Well, I hope she's okay, so I guess I'll see you later?"

"Not likely. I won't be at the club until the weekend."

"Oh, okay...guess I'll see you this weekend then."

"Okay, bye." *Click!* She hangs up before he could utter another word. "Damn, why it gotta be like dat?"

Ranetta pulls into the checkout area at Grady, then Mable and Val walk to the car. Val has a bouquet of flowers and a couple of balloons in her hand. Mable smiles and waves at Ranetta as she approaches. They both jump into the Benz, and she pulls off. "Hello, ladies."

"Hey, Netta, thanks for the balloons! See the flowers Ms. Thomas got for me? Aren't they pretty?"

Mable quickly says, "Yep, just like you!"

Val blushes as she quips, "Aw, thank you!"

Ranetta gushes, "That's so true! So where do you ladies want to eat? It's on me?"

Val answers, "I really don't care. I'm just starved."

"Yeah, it doesn't matter to me either. Wherever you want to go, Ms. Gibbs."

"Oh, please call me Netta. All my friends call me that."

Smiling, she says, "Okay din, Netta!" They all laugh as she continued down the road to wherever.

Meanwhile, Calvin's at the club doing some sound checks as the band, Twilight Groove, rehearsed. He's tweaking the volumes on the control board when a familiar presence is felt behind him. Stopping momentarily, "Okay...what is it, Ben?"

The spirit blasts, "You know what it is, clown! Where is she?"

He jumps in his seat from the booming voice. "Something's come up, Ben! Yo...she's in the hospital. Ranetta won't tell me why, but it's something serious! It's outta my hands for right now."

"Bullshit! You better get her here somehow, someway! I told your ass you had until this weekend or else!"

Frustrated now, Calvin blasts back, "Look, damn it! There's nothin' I can do about it right now, got it?" Quickly realizing his mistake, he braces himself for a blow, but...nothing. "Okay, fine."

Shocked, Calvin takes a look around the room as he relaxes a little, then says in a cocky tone, "Yeah...yeah, you damn right it's fine!" *Pop!*

It's 4:30 p.m. now, Calvin and the band exit the club. He hops into his truck and attempts to start it—nothing! He goes to check under the hood, then eventually slams it down in frustration. He walks over and kicks the front left tire. Calvin leans on the front fender and pulls out his phone to call his cousin. "Hello?"

"Yo, cuz, you in the area?"

"Yeah, I'm around dah way. Whaddup?"

"I think the damn battery in my truck is dead."

"Oh...well, hell, cuz. I can come scoop you up. You gonna stop and get cha a new one?"

"Hell yeah, if it ain't too much trouble."

"Naw. I gotcha, cuz."

Ten minutes later, Rodney pulls up, and Calvin jumps in the car. As they're rolling down the street, "You thirsty, cuz? I'ma stop at dat EZEE GO up dah way."

"Hey, I'm just the passenger, dude. That's cool with me." They go right past the park Rodney was posted up doing his hustle this past weekend. He turns into the parking lot of the convenience store and parks near the entrance. They walk in completely oblivious to the shiny black Crown Vic parked two spaces over. Inside the store, they walk down one aisle as the dude who Rodney had a previous altercation with bops up the next one over. The dude approaches the checkout when he suddenly notices someone familiar and goes over to greet them. As they're hobnobbin', Rodney walks up to the checkout with his drink and bag of chips. Calvin's still at the beer cooler, trying to decide on what he wanted. Out of nowhere, some guy just beyond the two dudes talking yells out, "Hey, dawg, you got some mo' of dat shit?"

The dude stops talking to his friend and says, "Damn, partna, you ain't gotta front like dat! We can go outside, and I can take care of you."

The guy shakes his head and blurts, "Naww, not you, playa. I'm talkin' 'bout him!" He points to Rodney. The dude whirls around, and their eyes meet! Rodney freezes for a second or two, then immediately darts out the store as the clerk yells, "Hey, your stuff! You're leaving your stuff!"

The dude turns to his friend and says, "Roll with me!"

As they bounce, Calvin finally witnesses the scene but still doesn't know his cousin has left the building. Looking around as he eases up to the checkout counter, he sets his beer down, thinking to himself, *Damn, where's cuz?* He peers out the front windows just in time to see his cousin's car flying out the parking lot, then seconds later, the black Crown Vic closing in fast! "What the fuck!" Calvin takes off out the door and makes a futile attempt to run after him.

Minutes before, Ranetta drops Mable off at her house, then she and Val head home. "Oh, I forgot to ask you about your trip. Did you and this mystery friend have a good time?"

"Yes, it was cool. The mountains are so nice, and it was very serene up there."

Val starts to giggle.

"Okay...so what's so funny, missy?"

"Umm-hmm, I bet it was! So much so that y'all got a hotel room."

Ranetta sighs, "Hold on...let's get something straight. This mystery guy is my boss, Floyd. That's right...Don't say nothin'!" She points her finger at her as she says it. "He had his own bed, and I had mine. I just met the man, honey!"

"Okay, okay...I'm sorry! Like I need to talk. Hell, I got into a car with a guy I didn't even know really and you see what happened to me."

"No...Look, Val. I didn't mean to say all that to make you feel bad. Everyone makes mistakes. It's something I know you'll never do again."

"Huh...you got that right."

Meanwhile, the chase is on! Rodney is weaving in and out of traffic. His phone is blowing up, but he doesn't answer. It's Calvin trying desperately to see what the hell is going on. The Crown Vic closes in on his tail and bumps him! Rodney looks in his rearview mirror, when the dude and his passenger instantly flash guns! He floors it, accelerating even more dangerously down the street. He barely misses a pedestrian trying to cross! The Crown Vic accelerates and is right back on his tail. Now come the gunshots. *Pop! Pop! Pop! Pop!* Bullets pierce the back windshield of the Honda, and glass shatters as Rodney screams, "*Oh shit!*" With the lightning-fast bullets barely missing him, the Crown Vic maneuvers to the left into oncoming traffic in an attempt to pull up close. Cars are honking and dodging out of the way as they continue on their deadly course!

Coming up over the hill in the opposite direction, Ranetta and Val are still conversing. "So I have to ask...Are you still gonna try to sing? The reason why I ask is because Calvin called me earlier today wondering if you would come to the club and rehearse with the new band. I told him you were in no condition to do that right now. Oh, and don't worry, I didn't tell him what happened. It's none of his business."

Val looks forward and exclaims, "You're right but—*watch out, Netta!*" She looks straight ahead and jerks the car just in the nick of time, avoiding a head-on collision with the Crown Vic speeding past! The Benz fishtails and spins out of control, then hits the curb and smashes into a phone pole. The driver and passenger side air bags instantly deploy. Ranetta and Val are jolted forward, plowing into the bags with intense force. Ranetta's nose is broken, and Val's face ends up even more bruised than it already was! Both started to cough and wheeze from the smoke caused by the airbags.

All the while, the Crown Vic had to swerve back into the right lane, causing Rodney to be cut off and take a sharp cut to his right, then jump the curb. He sails down a deep embankment and crashes into a ditch. The black car comes to a screeching halt, then backs up to the point where the Honda goes off the road and stops. The dude driving jumps out with a gun in hand and takes off down the hill. Totally stunned but not completely knocked out after hitting the steering wheel, Rodney sits back in his seat in a daze. Finally, he turns to witness a nine-millimeter pointing right at him! Rodney's eyes widened as he attempts to let out a scream, but too late. *Bam! Bam! Bam!* Rodney Clemens finished at the age of twenty-nine!

Ten minutes later, sirens sound in the area. Ranetta sits back in the driver's seat still in a daze as blood trickled from her nose. She looks over at Val, who has tears streaming down her face. "Oh no, Netta. You're bleeding!"

"I'll be fine, child. It's just a broken nose. It'll heal. It could've been worse!"

A group of bystanders has gathered around the car now. One of them knocks on the driver's side window. Ranetta opens the door, then the guy asks, "I saw what happened. Just sit tight. I called for help. The rescue should be here shortly. Here come the cops now, thank God!"

The police cruiser pulls up with lights flashing, and a minute later, a rescue pulls through but does not stop! It eventually arrives at the curb where Rodney's car went off the road. There's a group of people at that vantage point, looking down the hill. Police are telling them to move back to give room for the paramedics as they make their way down the hill. Several officers are sweeping the wooded area just beyond the crash. An eyewitness at the top of the hill tells one of the officers what she saw, "I seen this black guy jump out of a black Crown Victoria with black rims and tinted windows. He had a gun in his hand and took off down the hill in a hurry. Next thing I know, there were three shots! That's when I ran across the street! Another black guy gets out of the passenger side after that happened and yelled out something to him. I couldn't make out what he said, but shortly after that, the other dude appears back up the hill. Both of them get back in the car and peel off down the street."

"Were you able to get the license plate number?"

"Oh, no…when I heard those gunshots, I bolted immediately and stayed out of sight while I called y'all on my phone! Truth be told, I didn't even think to look."

"That's alright. As long as you're safe! So can you describe them? You know, what did they look like, what were they wearing?"

"Well…I remember the one with the gun was tall with braids. He had on a blue T-shirt and sagging blue jeans. Yeah, they were sagging because when he ran toward the car, he was holding them up like you see these guys do all the time. Anyway, the other dude was kinda muscular, with a real short haircut, and had on a red T-shirt with really baggy black jeans. That's all I can remember."

"Hey, I really appreciate all the info! This will definitely help us. We have somewhere to start, at least. Thank you, um…Ms.?"

"Oh, my name's Susan Collins."

By this time, Ranetta and Val are talking to the police as another rescue finally pulls up to the scene. The paramedics jump out and immediately start to assist both women. Val asks one of the officers, "Were y'all able to catch that fool that ran us off the road?"

"No, unfortunately not at the moment. I just got word though that we've got a pretty good lead on the suspects."

"Suspects? So there was more than one clown in the car? Wow, were they being chased or something?"

"Hey, all that I can tell you is that they were chasing someone, and it ended up in a fatality."

"Oh my god!"

"Yep, we've got an APB out on the black Crown Victoria now."

Val pauses for a moment, as she goes into deep thought, "A black Crown Vic? That's the same type of car I got thrown out of!" Then she asks the officer, "Did it have shiny black rims?"

Puzzled, the officer answers, "That I don't know…Umm, have you seen this car before?"

"Ahh…no, I don't think so. I just happened to notice that before we were run off the road."

"Oh…well, that is a good tip, though." He radios down to an officer at the homicide case. "Rick, do you copy?"

"Come in."

"One of the ladies involved in the accident down here noticed that the perps' car had shiny black rims on it. You copy?"

"Duly noted, thanks."

"Ten-four." A slight rage begins to build in Val now, her mind racing again. *Oh…I guess since those bastards didn't kill me the first time, they're provided with a second opportunity? Huh…well, there won't be a third. They can best believe that!* She climbs into the rescue with Ranetta, and they're off to the hospital yet again!

Calvin finally gets off the bus at the entrance of the subdivision where his cousin's house dwells. As he walks down the street, he's thinking, "Man, what the hell happened today? I've called this brotha several times! Nothin'!" He gets into the house and checks the answering machine. No messages! He shrugs and starts to figure, "Hell, he'll call sooner or later. I'll deal with that damn truck later on!" He says all this out loud. He decides to cook something to eat and sit down to some television. Calvin channel surfs and catches the news as they're about to go to break, giving a glimpse of the stories coming up. "Man fatally shot today after a high-speed car chase. Police are looking for a black Ford Crown Victoria with black rims and tinted windows. Anybody with information, please contact authorities immediately but do not approach! Perp is said to be armed and dangerous!"

He almost chokes on his food as he blurts out loud, "What the fuck! Oh…hell no!" He sits back in his seat, totally stunned. Soon the commercial break is over, and the anchorwoman begins the report. "A black male in his late twenties was gunned down at point-blank range today. According to authorities, it was after being chased by two other unknown black males in a 2004 to 2007 model black Ford Crown Victoria with custom black rims and tinted windows. The incident occurred in East Atlanta near Cleveland Avenue. The identity of the man murdered is withheld by authorities pending an investigation, as well as to contacting family members first. The perpetrators' identities are still unknown at the moment but are considered armed and dangerous. An APB has been put out on the car. We'll have more details as they develop…Coming up next, we'll talk to a woman who nearly had a head-on collision with the madmen in the—"

Click. Calvin turns off the TV and begins to sulk, knowing deep down in his heart that the person she was talking about was his cousin.

The next morning, two detectives knock at his door, confirming his hunch. Calvin peeks out the window, then slowly opens the front door. "Hello, I'm Detective Lockett, and this is my partner, Detective Jolson." They both display their badges as Lockett continues, "Are you Rudolph Clemens Jr.?"

"No, sir, that's my uncle. My name's Calvin Kitchen."

"Oh…well, is he around? We'd like to talk to him."

"Actually, no…he's been living in Florida for the past two years. He's been letting my cousin Rodney stay here. I just moved here last week from Kansas City, Missouri."

Detective Jolson asks, "So you're the only other person living here now?"

"Yep…it's just me and my cousin." Hoping deep down that maybe they actually had some good news, but he really knew that wasn't the case. And just like he thought, Detective Lockett drops his head, and Jolson looks away for a moment. Then he continues to explain, "I hate to tell you, but you *are* the only one that's living here now. Unfortunately, your cousin, Rodney was shot and killed yesterday after a high-speed chase. We're still looking for the two perpetrators."

Calvin hangs his head, and tears start to flow. Barely getting his words out, he says, "I…I…I had a feelin' when I heard the madness on the news yesterday. I didn't really want to believe it. Oh damn! I was with him before it all happened! I couldn't figure out what the hell was goin' on though!"

Jolson asks, "What exactly do you mean? When were you with him?"

"First off, he stopped by to pick me up from work. The battery in my truck was dead. We were on our way to get a new one when he decided to stop at an EZEE GO. I can't remember what street it was on…Anyway, we stopped and went in to get something to drink. I'm over at the beer cooler tryin' to decide what I wanted when I noticed him walking toward the checkout counter. When I finally got there, I looked around trying to see where he was, and the next thing I know, he's flyin' out the parking lot being chased by this black car with tinted windows and black shiny rims!"

Lockett asks, "Can you recall if the perps were in the store prior to the chase?"

He shrugs and continues to sulk a bit. "Man, I don't know! Unfortunately, I wasn't payin' attention like dat. I assume so, yeah."

"Well, see, that info will help tremendously because we can seize those surveillance tapes."

Jolson adds, "Yeah, if we could view the tape and analyze it, maybe we could determine exactly who the suspects are. Can you recall at least the vicinity?"

"It was somewhere near Cleveland Avenue."

Jolson nods his head, and Lockett extends his hand, then says, "That's a good start. Thanks a lot, Mr. Kitchen, and my condolence to you."

Jolson pats him on the shoulder, "Yes, same here, buddy. We'll be in touch with you about any more information, as well as any important questions we may have, okay?"

Calvin simply nods as the detectives make their way back to the unmarked sedan parked out front. As they disappear down the street, he stands in the doorway looking pitiful, not knowing what to do next.

Thursday afternoon comes around, and Rudolph arrives in Atlanta. He drove up with another nephew of his, Thomas, and his girlfriend, Roxanne. They stop by the house to pick up Calvin and make their way to the morgue to officially identify Rodney. They're at a traffic stop, and a car pulls up beside them bumping loud music. Calvin happens to look over and does a double take! It's a black Crown Victoria with tinted windows and black rims!

Now enraged, Calvin thinks, *I don't believe this shit! I thought for sure these dumbass niggas would dump the car somewhere out of sight! Really? I know it's them, gotta be!* He doesn't say anything to anybody in the car. They were already distraught as it is; he didn't want to complicate things any further. Plus, he wasn't completely sure. As he continues in his thoughts, his rage builds. *Scum! These bold-ass, low-down, dirty, scumbags! They're rollin' around town like it ain't shit!* The light turns green, and they proceed down the block. The Crown Vic peels off, but before it disappeared, he manages to get the license plate number. Now he's pissed off even more because he actually had the nerve to have a vanity plate. It reads, "DA DUNC."

"What the fuck! 'Da Dunc'?" He's completely quiet now, secretly fuming the rest of the way to the morgue.

The Guilty One

After informing the police later that afternoon with the plate number, Calvin finally gets a call that evening. They found out the owner's name was Latrell Duncan. He had a prior conviction for drug possession back in 2005. The police also revealed that Mr. Duncan has disappeared, and APB has been issued. "We'll keep you posted if there's any more breaks in the case, Mr. Kitchen, and thanks for the important lead." He hangs up as Rudolph walks into the living room with two bottles of beer in hand, then passes one to Calvin as he says, "Welp, just got off the phone with Pastor Rolland, and the funeral is set for this Saturday at Keep Hope Baptist Church. He'll be laid to rest at the Foster Roads Memorial Cemetery here in Decatur." Calvin takes a long sip of his beer before saying, "Wow, I still can't believe this is real! My cuz is really gone...and just like that!"

Rudolph takes a sip and replies, "Neph, what the hell happened? Was he in some kinda trouble wit dim? Was it an argument dat got outta hand? I mean, goddamn, he was shot at point-blank range for Pete's sake! It wasn't a damn robbery because po-po said dey didn't take anything!" Shaking his head, he replies, "Hell, all I know, Unk, is a couple of dudes chased him down in a black car, Rod crashed, and one of them bastards shot him to death! I don't know what caused it, and it may have been an attempted robbery or simply revenge...I don't know!"

"Why would you say revenge?"

"I said it because everything that's happened is so out of the blue and could very well be a possibility. I don't even know these dudes, and truth be told...don't even know all of Rod's history. He might've known them...Don't know!" Rudolph shakes his head in complete disgust and finishes off his beer.

It's Friday afternoon as Ranetta jumps out of a cab and enters Club Boozy's with her nose bandaged up. She greets Floyd, and he gives her a hug, then gently holds her face, looking her over. "Wow... it's not too bad. I certainly hope they catch the assholes who caused this!"

"Huh...I do too! Any luck on new info about the robbery?"

"No...nothing at all! I'm not worried about that right now, though. I'm more concerned about you and your niece. By the way... how is she? Will she be coming back?"

"Yeah...eventually. She needs a little time to get her confidence back."

"Hey, I understand...she can come back whenever she's ready." All of a sudden, the lights begin to flicker on and off. Floyd blurts, "Oh lord! Not this shit again! The power company came out last time and couldn't find anything wrong. I guess I'll go call this electrician I know. Maybe he can pinpoint the problem...at least I hope." As he's about to walk away, "Hey...if you're hungry, you can go in the kitchen and get Susan to hook you up with somethin'."

"Oh, okay...that sounds good. I'll do that." She heads toward the back, as he goes upstairs to his office. Now...the lights stop flickering.

Calvin's sitting in the living room at his uncle's house, chatting with him, Thomas, Roxanne, and an old friend of Rudolph's named Harvey when the phone rings. Rudolph answers, "Hello?" There's a female voice, "Hello...is Calvin around?"

"Yeah...hold on. Cal, telephone." He stands and reaches out to hand him the phone. "Hello?"

"Hey, Cal, so who was that? What...y'all havin' a party and didn't invite me?" As she's laughing, "No...we're definitely not doin' that. That was my uncle Rudolph, so how you doin'?"

"Man...I need somethin' to calm my nerves! Yo...is Rod around? Shoot...I need some of that good stuff right now."

"*What?* Are you out of your damn mind? You can't be serious now! Child...considering what you've just been through...that's the last thing that needs to be on your mind!" Realizing he's creating a scene now, he quickly blurts, "Wait a minute...hold on!" He excuses himself from the room and goes out to the front steps before continuing the call. "Val, look…Rod's dead!"

"*Dead?* What? Oh my god! When?"

"Tuesday! He was chased by some shitheads, and one of them shot 'im point-blank range! Dey murdered him!"

"No, no, no, no! Oh my god! I can't believe it! It was *him* who died? Oh shit!" She starts to whine hysterically as Calvin, confused, asks, "What the hell you talkin' about…It was him who died? Why would you ask that?"

"Because it was probably the freakin' car that ran Netta and me off the road! The police said they were chasin' someone at the time! That…the person was shot afterward!" Val breaks down completely now, crying uncontrollably. "Wow…I had no idea dat y'all were in the mix. Damn!"

"I'm sorry, Cal…I didn't mean to be rude like that. Please give my condolences to the rest of the family."

"Hey…it's okay. If you want to, come to the funeral tomorrow at one o'clock. Call me later, and I'll give you the directions."

"Alright, I'll do that…bye."

Calvin's mind races now as he stands there dumbfounded. "Damn…I think I know why cuz got killed! That coke we was snortin' was probably stolen! That would explain why he got back so late that night. It also explains why that dude down the way got capped. Them clowns thought it was my cousin's car! Oh shit!"

Back at the club, Floyd finishes talking to the electrician and hangs up. As he was about to stand, suddenly there's a "Psst" out of nowhere! Stunned, he frantically gazes around the room and yells, "Who's that?"

Nothing! Seconds later, again, "Psst."

Now a bit more agitated, he blurts, "Okay, damn it! Enough with the games!" He looks under his desk, then tries the door behind it. The lock was already replaced and intact. Then…"Calvin did it!" in a faint yet distinct whisper.

Floyd instantly jumps out of his chair and shouts, "What? Who the hell is sayin' that?"

The voice whispers again, "Calvin did it! It was Calvin! Calvin! Calvin! Cal—"

He interrupts, "This shit ain't funny now! Who's sayin' that? I know I'm not crazy!" He sits back down and opens one of the drawers of his desk. Floyd then reaches in and puts his hand on the nine-millimeter that was stashed there.

"Calvin took your money. It was Calvin! He took it all…Boozy."

Enraged, Floyd takes his gun out, stands, and yells, "*Goddammit!* Who the fuck are you? What are you talkin' about? Calvin? That son of a bitch!"

Now the voice, no longer whispering, says, "Put the gun away, asshole! It's of no use to you right now."

Continuing to look confused, he asks, "Where are you? Show yourself."

The spirit slowly reveals itself. "Where did you come from? Why the fuck are you messin' with me?"

The spirit laughs and says, "Damn, Boozy…you don't remember me? The man you swiped money from back in KC?"

He ponders for a moment, then looks up in total shock, "Ben? Benny Tucket? What the hell!"

Laughing again, the spirit answers, "Yeah…you got it! And that's a place I plan on taking a few people to, shortly. Yes…yes, it's me, Boozy! Surprise, surprise…but now before you go pop dat asshole, I need you to bring him here to me…we got some unfinished business to take care of, dig?"

"What kind of business?"

"Don't worry about that! You just make sure that clown shows up!"

Frowning, Floyd blurts, "Who the hell are you ordering me around like that? Besides, I'll handle dat muthafucka myself!" He waves the gun in the air as he says it.

"No…I can get you your money back without resorting to a mess like that! If you kill 'im…how the hell ya gonna get your loot back, huh? Just scare the shit out of 'im, but don't do 'im! I got something better planned."

Floyd puts the gun back and closes the drawer. "Alright…but I need my money back pronto!"

Down in the kitchen, Susan and Ranetta chat over lunch. "Oh my god! I had no idea that was you and your niece in the car crash up the way! I didn't catch that part on the news. I was so preoccupied with what was going on at the murder scene. Wow!"

"Yep…it was us. We survived, and that's all that matters."

"You're exactly right about that, but you know what though? I did get a good look at the two guys."

Shocked, Ranetta asks, "Are you serious?"

"Yeah."

"So…if you were to see a lineup, you would be able to pick them out?"

"Yeah…I think so."

"Good…I hope they get some suspects to show you! Those bastards definitely need to be taken off the streets!" Shaking her head in agreement, Susan says, "I still don't know what it was about. Some are speculating it was over drugs."

"Hell…I wouldn't doubt it." Ranetta's cellphone rings. "Hello?"

Val sniffs and says, "Hey, Netta."

"Uh-oh…now what's wrong?"

"I found out the guy who was killed in the accident we were involved in was Calvin's cousin."

"What! Oh my god…you mean the one he's stayin' with or was at least?"

"Yes."

"Damn it…so how's he doin'? Well, I guess I need to call him."

"He seems to be okay. Umm…he's with his uncle and some other people. He told me the funeral is tomorrow at one and that I can call him later for directions."

"Okay…Wow…umm…so sorry to hear this! When it rains, it pours."

"Yep, it seems that's how it's gone, lately. There's something else…something I didn't tell you before. You know the car I was thrown out of…well, I have a strong feeling it's the same one that ran us off the road."

"Are you serious? The cook here at the club, Susan…said that she got a good look at those two monsters! I hope and pray they catch these assholes for sure now! Oh my god!"

"What did they look like?" She hears Ranetta ask Susan, and her response was, "The one driving the car was a tall, black guy with braids and—"

Val interrupts, "That's one of them! That's the one that was driving that night. I just know it! Oh my god!" She starts to have a slight anxiety attack, shivering thinking about the horrid event again.

"Oh lord…Val, please calm down. The only thing we can do now is wait and see what the cops do."

Val calms down a bit and agrees, but in the back of her mind, she thinks, *Someone…better yet, all of them are gonna pay for what they've done!*

It's six o'clock now, two hours before the club opens, and Calvin gives Floyd a call to let him know he wasn't going to make it in. "Hello?"

"Hey, Boozy, my man…umm…I'm not gonna be in tonight. I've had a loss in the family…umm…my cousin was murdered and—"

Floyd interrupts, "Yeah, yeah, I've heard! So sorry to hear it, man!" Still raging inside, he tries desperately to sound sympathetic. He's really thinking to himself, Yeah, yeah…what-the-fuck-ever, bitch ass! He's not gonna be the only one murdered if I don't get my money back!"

"Oh. I appreciate that, man…umm…The funeral is tomorrow."

"Well, hey…take all the time you need. I'll catch up with you soon."

"Real soon!" he thought. "Once again, thanks, man. I appreciate everything!" Then Calvin hangs up. Floyd reaches into his desk drawer and pulls out the nine, then leaves his office. He strolls over to Byron's office to see him working diligently on something. "BW…I'm gonna step out for a bit. Hold it down until I get back. I should be here by the time we open, alright?"

"Alright, big chief, no problem."

As Floyd's rolling down the street, he calls Calvin. "Hello."

"Yo, Cal…whatcha doin' right now?"

"Oh…umm…nothin' really. What's up?"

"Oh, nothin' much, man. I just wanted to holla at cha…ahh… maybe buy you a drink and somethin' to eat. My treat for sure…I mean, considering what you've been through these last couple of days." There's slight hesitation, then he replies, "Okay…umm…do you want me to meet you somewhere?"

"Yeah, where are you?"

"I'm at home."

"What's the address? I've got a navigation system, so I'll find you."

"Actually, I really don't want to do that. Umm…you know this is my uncle's house, and my family's really funny about those types of things. You know what I'm sayin'?"

"Oh, okay…no problem. I'll meet you somewhere then." Floyd just smirks, nodding his head up and down. "I'm actually near a train station. I think it's called Kensington? I'ma hop on a bus right quick and meet you there, okay?"

"Cool…Kensington station it is! I'll see you in a few."

"Cool, see ya!" Floyd says to himself, "Damn…seems kinda suspicious of his ass to not want me to pick him up at his place! Who would rather pay and deal with MARTA instead of being picked up for free? A guilty muthafucka, that's who!"

He finally arrives at the station and scoops Calvin up. They decided to venture to a soul food joint that was nearby. After they put in their order, Floyd began, "So hey…ahh…I never got a chance to ask you…ahh…Where were you when my place got hit?"

Calvin was obviously thrown by this question because he hesitated before answering, "Wow…umm, I wasn't expecting you to ask me anything like that, at least, not now anyway! But to answer the question, I was at home, chillin'."

Floyd smirks as he notices Calvin's body language. He witnesses a certain uneasiness after the long pause. "Okay, that's good. Hey, just had to ask. Hell, I've asked everyone else already."

Calvin smoothly says, "Oh…so there hasn't been a break in the case? Wow."

"Nope, not a damn thing! But I'm optimistic! I have a feelin' that I'll get my money back…real soon!" With a surprised look on his face, Calvin asks, "Huh…get your money back? What…you… ahh…suspect someone?" Now the waitress arrives with their drinks. Floyd's having a whiskey sour, while Calvin has a rum and Coke. Floyd takes a sip, then answers, "No, not for sure yet, but I'm getting close." He shoots him a slight glare, winks, and takes another sip of his drink. "Well…who?"

"Seriously, can't say right now…Anyway, how are the funeral arrangements comin'? Do you need any help?"

Bewildered now, he says, "No, umm…everything's squared away…umm…but thanks!"

"Cool." Now their food arrives, and they eat in silence. Calvin's wondering, *What the hell does this cat know? I'ma have to keep my eye on this joker!*

Floyd's in deep thought as he chows down, *Yep…I'm gonna cut this son of a bitch down! That muthafuckin' Ben better have somethin' good planned, I know that!* His very last thought brought him to ask this, "Oh yeah…do you remember Benny Tucket?"

Calvin damn near chokes on his food before he could muster, "What!" He coughs as he continues, "What made you ask about him of all people?"

"I don't know…Maybe it's because I remember back in KC, I hit that clown up for twenty g's and escaped to Chicago to lay low for a couple of years. Then I decided to move here and set up my operations. Part of dat loot helped me get started, so you know…it seems like karma's a bitch, maybe? I don't know!"

"Wow, I didn't know all of that." Calvin picks up a napkin and wipes his mouth while staring crazily at Floyd as he continued to enjoy his meal.

Leaving the restaurant now, they both walk down the sidewalk toward Floyd's car. Suddenly, a flatbed truck passes by with a half-burnt black Crown Victoria on the back. Calvin immediately notices the scorched black rims. The truck stops at the traffic light. He trots out into the street to get a glimpse at the license plate. Sure enough, just as he thought, it read, "DA DUNC." He stands there shaking his head as the truck starts to pull off. Now there's a loud horn blaring behind him. Startled, he jumps and turns around to see he's holding up traffic. He throws his hands up and runs out of the way. When he gets back to the sidewalk, Floyd's looking at him like he's crazy. "Damn, man, what the hell was that all about?"

He just smirks and says, "Can't say right now." Then Calvin abruptly strolls down the sidewalk as Floyd just glares at him.

The Setup

It's Saturday afternoon. Calvin and the rest of the family are gathered at the house for lunch. He breaks away for a moment to call Detective Lockett about the murder case. "Hello, Detective Lockett, this is Calvin Kitchen. I was wonderin'…how's the case goin'?"

"Actually, I'm glad you called, Mr. Kitchen. We were able to pinpoint the EZEE GO you and your cousin went to and got to view the surveillance tapes. Mr. Duncan and his accomplice were there, talking. We saw your cousin run out of the store first, then Duncan and his friend followed. We now know his name's Derrick Sampson. He also has a prior conviction, but for assault and battery. He's been on probation, and I would say he's definitely in violation! We've put out a definite warrant for his ass! Like I said to you before, we'll keep you posted if anything else comes up."

"Oh, yeah…I know you will, and as a matter of fact, I was walkin' out of a restaurant last night and saw that Crown Vic I told you about on a flatbed, all burnt up. Ahh…do you know about that?"

"Yep, they ditched it in a secluded area in Stone Mountain. They torched it, of course, trying to get rid of evidence. How did you know that was the one?"

"I saw the license plate."

The detective laughs and says, "Yeah…stupid, huh?"

"Ya damn right. I just shook my head when I saw that!"

"Well, these criminals out here aren't the brightest, I tell ya! But again, as I've said, we'll keep you in the loop as much as we can. If you don't hear from me in the next couple of days, feel free to call, alright?"

"Will do. Thank you."

"No problem, Mr. Kitchen. Talk to you later." Calvin goes back to his lunch with the family before they have to make their way to the church.

As they're pulling up to New Hope Baptist Church, Calvin's surprised to see Val standing outside waiting. He gets out and greets her at the entrance. "Wow, I didn't hear from you today. I figured you'd changed your mind."

"No, I really wanted to show my support. Man, it's such a tragedy!"

He nods his head in agreement and puts an arm around her, then they walk in together.

During the service, he couldn't help but feel guilty all of a sudden. Looking over at Val as tears streamed down her face, he knew right then that he couldn't go through with the previous plans. He already had the money, so the next task would have to be keeping her as far away from the club as possible. *But how?* His mind races because he knew he couldn't go back his damn self!. *Oh no…what about Netta?* He reaches over and grabs her hand as tears begin to flow. Val looks over and grabs his hand tightly. She nods as she immediately focuses her attention back to the pastor who continues to give a heartwarming sermon.

Later, the pallbearers place the coffin into the hearse as the family gets into the limo that was parked behind it. Calvin motions for Val to join them and then they're off. Now a little less emotional, he asks Val, "Hey, how's Netta doin'?"

"She's doin' okay, tryin' to stay busy. You know how it is. You stay busy to keep your mind off your problems. She told me to tell you that she's sorry for your loss and that she has you and your family in her prayers."

"Tell her I said thanks, and I hope she gets well soon. I also wanted to tell you that there's no rush at all to go back to the club. In fact…umm…I don't think I'm goin' back."

With a bewildered look on her face, Val asks, "Why? Where else are you gonna go? I have to do something. I can't keep livin' off of Netta! We've got rent to pay and everything else."

"I'll be alright. I got a little something stashed away. I can help you!"

Val smiles. "Thanks, Cal, but that's not necessary. I can manage."

He's shaking his head as he says, "Look, I have to tell you something about that place that's not right! Not right at all!"

Frowning, she asks, "Like what? What's wrong?"

"Well...I can't talk about it right now, Val."

They approach the Foster Roads Memorial Cemetery and proceed down a long winding road until they reach the spot where Rodney Lamond Clemens will be laid to rest. Soon, everyone gathers and listens to the final eulogy. Some prayed while others wept. Calvin stands with his uncle, cousin, and the rest of the family as they bid their last farewell. Val hung back, teary-eyed, taking it all in.

Meanwhile, back at the club, "So what the fuck you gonna do, Boozy?" blasts the spirit.

"Look, damn it! I got this shit under control, Ben! He's at his cousin's funeral right now, okay? I'm gonna go and get him later, then bring his ass here! He *will* be here, tonight, I promise!"

"He better!" He vanishes as Floyd storms out of the office. He trots down the stairs and promptly leaves the club. He makes his way to his SUV and jumps in. Floyd starts to back out and immediately has to slam on the brakes! A white Chevy Caprice swerves out of the way and screeches to a halt. A tall black dude with braids pops out of the driver's side with a mean scowl and spreads his arms apart. Looking back, Floyd just sighs, drops his head, puts the SUV in park, then turns it off. He grabs for something from his dashboard, exits, and walks to the back, saying, "Sorry, sorry, dude...my fault! I wasn't payin' attention!"

"Damn, old man, you in a hurry or somethin'?"

"No, not really. I just got some shit on my mind, but anyway, I got some free passes here to getting into the club if you're interested." He holds them up in the air, showing them.

The dude shakes his head and laughs as he replies, "Alright din, man, dat's cool! How many you got?"

"How many do you need?"

The dude looks down into the car, and the person on the passenger side says something. He looks back up at Floyd and says, "We need four."

"I got cha." He hands the four passes to him. The dude nods, then jumps back in the car and jets off down the block. Floyd gets back into his SUV and this time, slowly backs out and proceeds.

After being dropped off back at the church, Val jumps into the rental car Ranetta got after the accident. She needed a good drink after the sad occasion, so she decided to go to the local liquor store. She goes in and immediately makes her way to one of the back coolers. Gazing at the endless selection of wines, she settles on a bottle of chardonnay. As Val reaches in to retrieve it, she stops cold and stares at the reflections of the four men who just entered the store in the glass of the cooler door. Latrell Duncan, Derrick Sampson, Ricky Brannen, and Stan McTiernan ramble on as she keeps a close eye on them. She grabs the bottle and nonchalantly walks up to the checkout counter, looking in their direction only once. As the clerk was ringing her up, she heard one of them exclaim, "Oh damn…what the…Man, is dat…yeaahh!" Her eyes widen, and her heart sinks! "Damn, I've been lookin' fo' dis, cuz! Dis the drink I've been tellin' y'all about!"

She closes her eyes and breathes a sigh of relief! This is just as the clerk told her the amount she owed. "Ahh, ma'am, that's $10.99?"

Startled, she opens her eyes, quickly pays, and promptly leaves the store without looking back. Val sits for a moment, waiting on the guys to come out of the store. Strolling out eventually, they approach the white Caprice that was parked one space over from her. She heard one of them ask, "Yo, dawg…them passes to Big Boozy's, was they fo' tonight?"

Latrell answers, "Yeah, cuz, let's flow on up through there. I need tah pick up a ho tonight, my nigga…Ya feel me?"

All were in agreement, laughed, and high-fived one another, then piled into the car and vamoosed. Val frowns hard as she gazed in the car's direction as it pulls out of the parking lot. She starts her car, while plotting her next move. Revenge was definitely in the forecast!

Shortly after Calvin arrives home, he gets a call from Floyd.

"Hey, Cal, you hangin' in there, buddy? I know it's been a hel- luva day, but I was wondering if I could meet you somewhere? I've got this CD I want you to hear. This cat wants to sing at the club, and he burned some of his original stuff on it. I could really use your opinion, and I won't hold you long at all."

Hesitant, Calvin says, "Yeah, okay, for a little while. I need to recharge…get my mind off things. When and where?"

"How about seven thirty at the same train station I picked you up last time?"

"Alright, I'll see you then."

"Cool…I'll see ya!" Calvin goes to his room and closes the door. He reaches under his bed and pulls out a briefcase that was hidden there. He places it on the bed, unlocks it, flips the top up, and stares at the neatly stacked rows of money inside.

Calvin says to himself, "Damn…I might have to hide this shit somewhere else! Somewhere accessible, though, just in case I have to jump ship right quick! I can get it and go." He ponders on this for a moment, then simply shrugs, closes the briefcase, and slides it back under the bed.

Meanwhile, Val rummages through her closet trying to pick out an outfit to wear to Club Boozy's. Her plan was to get those bastards busted and disgusted tonight! Her first priority when she arrived was to see Susan. "Having two positive IDs should do the trick. I wish I had a gun, then there would be no mistakes! Of course, I'll be the one going to jail. So actually, not a good idea." Finally finding the outfit she wanted, she continues to ponder her next moves.

Unsuspecting Revenge

It's 7:35 p.m. as Floyd pulls into the train station parking lot. He spots Calvin and toots his horn. Calvin runs over and jumps in. "Boozy, my man, how's it goin'?"

In kind of a dry voice, he says, "Oh, everything's lovely."

As they're rolling along, Calvin asks, "So who's this cat you wanted me to listen to? Is he a local act, brand new in the business, or what?"

"I guess you could say he's got some experience. He sounds good to me. Let's just say this…your opinion or what you got to say is vital to your life…*motherfucka*!" Floyd immediately points the nine-millimeter he had hidden by his side right at him!

"What *the hell* is this shit, Floyd? Why are you pointing a damn gun at me? Is this some kind of sick joke?"

"*Hell no*, this ain't no joke! We goin' to the club right now and settle this shit once and for all!"

"Settle what, Floyd?"

"We'll talk about that when we get there. For right now, shut the fuck up!"

Calvin's mind is reeling now. Even scared out of his wits, he still has the nerve to ask more questions. "Man, why you gotta go there? Hey, I thought I was supposed to be listening to some cat singin'?"

"Shut up! I just told your dumb ass that to get you right where you're sittin'…partna!"

"What is this all about, Boozy?"

"Didn't I just tell you to shut up? That's *Mr. Clinton* from here on out…ya got it, clown? Only my real friends call me Boozy!"

It was complete silence all the way to the club after that.

Val pulls into the club's parking lot at 7:50 p.m., finds a spot, and backs into the space. She sits, waiting and watching. Shortly, the lot begins to fill up at 8:15 p.m. Floyd drives up and parks on the side of the building. Still pointing the gun, he motions for Calvin to get out. "Very slowly, nigga! If you run, I'll drop yo' ass immediately… *got it?*"

Calvin nervously nods and exits the vehicle. Floyd gets out and quickly points the gun at him again. He motions him toward the side door. Calvin slowly makes his way there with Floyd on his heels. Once there, he says, "Okay…now step aside and stand right there. Don't you move a muscle, *dig?*"

He complies, and Floyd unlocks the door. Unnoticed, they make their way to the staircase leading up to his office.

Suddenly, a familiar voice behind them yells out, "Hey, Boozy, what's up? Oh…hey, Calvin, surprised to see you here."

Floyd quickly conceals the gun in his coat pocket but keeps it pointed at Calvin. He kind of glances back and says, "Oh…umm… what's up, BW? Aahh…just wanted ole Cal here to check out some new talent's material. We'll be up in my office. I'll be back out to check on things shortly, alright?"

"Yeah, okay, that's cool." He watches them turn and proceed up the steps with a confused look on his face. Byron shrugs it off, then makes his way to one of the bars to check on some supplies. The bartender, on the phone, sees him and waves him over. "Hey, Byron, there's someone here that wants to speak to a manager."

"Hello, this is Byron. How can I help you?"

"Hello, Byron…my name's Valencia. I'm Ranetta's niece."

"Oh yeah! How ya doin' this evening? You're supposed to be the one eventually singing here, right?"

"Yes, it's me…umm…is Susan around?"

"Nope, not tonight. I didn't schedule her to work until tomorrow. Do you want to leave a number? I can see to it that she gets it."

"Umm…no, that's okay. I already have her number. I tried to reach her earlier, but she didn't answer. I guess she'll eventually call me back. Thanks anyway."

"No problem…So how's Ranetta doing?"

"She's doin' alright…like me…anxious to get back to work."

"Well…whenever you ladies are ready, we'll be happy to have you back."

"Cool, thanks! I'm not gonna hold ya, but I'll probably see you later…I'm in the area."

"Great. See you later, then."

"Bye."

Now talking to herself, "Damn…I guess I'ma have to do this all by myself! That's fine…No matter what, those assholes are goin' down tonight!"

"Well, well, well…tried to play me, huh?" *Smack!* Calvin goes flying across the room. "See,…that's why yo' ass is grass!"

"Hey…*what the fuck, Ben!*" Floyd continues pointing his gun at him as he eases the office door closed. Calvin, on all fours, grimaces and manages to speak up, "No more than you tryin' to play me! I betcha you told this muthafucka I stole his money!"

The spirit laughs as it quipped, "Oh…I know you ain't tryin' to turn everything around on me! Where the hell is Val, *you son of a bitch?*"

"Hey, look, damn it! I don't give a rat's ass about any of y'all's drama right now! Where's my damn *money?* And wait, what does she have to do with anything?"

The spirit bellows, "Tell him, you miserable, slitherin' snake! Tell him about our deal!"

Calvin had to think quick! He didn't want to reveal that to Floyd, especially since he had that gun pointed at him, so he yells out, "If you wanna know where your money is, Floyd, ask this piece of shit of a ghost!" pointing his finger back into space.

"Awww…you conniving *jackass*, you lie!"

Meanwhile, it's 8:45 p.m., and the club was starting to fill up pretty good. The white Caprice finally pulls into the parking lot. Still parked, Val smirks as she spots the car. The four guys exit and stroll toward the entrance. Gathering her purse and cell phone, she eventually follows behind them, cautiously. She hangs back a bit and lets a group of people enter the club first. Once inside, the four find a table, sit, and instantly start to order drinks. Val finds a seat at one of the bars farthest away from them, but not so far she couldn't keep tabs on them. She immediately calls Susan. This time she answers, "Hello?"

"Hey, Susan, this is Valencia Tucket, Ranetta's niece."

"Oh, yeah...hey, did you try to call me earlier?"

"Yeah, that was me. I need a favor...umm...Do you remember the name and number of that detective who interviewed you about the murder case?"

"Wow, yes. I've got them around here somewhere...Why? What's up?"

"Those two bastards are here at the club along with the two other goons that I know for sure were involved in my rape case!"

"What! Oh my god! No, no, no...let me go find his card and I'll call you back, okay?"

She hangs up the phone before Val could answer. She sits her phone down and orders a drink. Looking in the guys' direction, she watches as they drink and chat. A group of ladies walk in searching for a table, and they start flirting with them.

Val thinks to herself, *Damn those good-for-nothing, trifling dogs! They're over there sizing up their next victims! Ooh, I can't wait.* Her thoughts are interrupted by the ring of her phone.

"Hello?"

"Hey, I called him and left a message. I told him it was urgent and left him your number. His name is Lamar Lockett, and his number is 707-482-2879. Please, *please* be careful, Val! You're not gonna confront them, are you?"

"Hell no...they don't even know I'm here!"

"Good. Keep me posted!"

"Oh, trust me, I will!"

She looks down at her phone and notices she has an incoming call. "Hey, Susan, I think this might be him on the other line. I'll call you back as soon as I finish." She switches over and hears a man's voice, "Hello, Ms. Tucket, are you there?"

"Yes, is this Detective Lockett?"

"Yeah, I received a message from a Susan Collins saying that you have urgent information regarding the murder case we've been working on."

"Yep, those two bastards are here along with two other dudes who brutalized and raped me!"

"What! Are you sure about all this, Ms. Tucket?"

"You damn right I'm sure!"

"Where are you?"

"I'm at Club Boozy's, downtown."

"Okay, okay, stay where you are! We're on the way! Do they know you're there?"

"No!"

"Good! Please do *not* say anything, understood? Just stay put!"

"I'm not goin' anywhere."

She hangs up and immediately calls Susan with the news. "Hey, girl, they're on the way!"

"Good, because I am too! I can't miss this! I'm already en route."

"Cool…I'll see you when you get here."

Smack! Calvin hits the floor once again! "Tell him, damn it! Tell him what the deal is, ya *coward!*"

Calvin pulls himself up on Floyd's desk and blurts, "There was no deal!"

Floyd explodes, "Look, I don't give a damn! I just want my money *now!*"

"Calm down, asshole. You'll get that money soon enough! First thing's first. I need the soul that's due to me!"

"What soul? What the hell are you talkin' 'bout?"

"Valencia!"

"Don't listen to him, Floyd!" Calvin starts to sob loudly.

"Oh yes…that was the deal. Her soul for your money. The deal was made way back in KC, after my club burned to the ground, courtesy of yours truly." The spirit starts to laugh devilishly as Floyd stood there, shocked.

"Please don't listen to him, Floyd! I'm beggin' you!" then he falls to his knees. Floyd ponders what was just laid on him as the laughter continued. Rage built inside him, then *bam!* He pistol-whipped Calvin straight in the jaw! The blow immediately sends him to the ground yet again. As he starts to aim the gun at him, it is mysteriously knocked from his grasp.

"Watch it, buddy! Don't do nothin' rash! At least not now...I still need this scumbag to bring her to me. Besides, how the fuck you gonna get your loot back?"

Calvin lunges at Floyd and knocks him on the floor. "Not in this lifetime!" Calvin jumps up and storms out the slightly opened door before the spirit got a chance to slam it shut. Nearly knocking over the nosy-ass cleaning lady who was just outside it. He dashes down the steps. Nosy Nancy is exactly what some of the people that worked at the club called her. She always seemed to be in or know everybody's business! She gathers herself and takes off running when the door flew open. Floyd exits the room with his gun in hand and Ben's spirit howling loudly, hot on his trail!

Val walks out of the restroom talking to Susan on the phone. "I'll meet you at the front entrance. I'm heading that way right now."

"Okay, cool. I'm looking for a spot to park as we speak." Suddenly, she's nearly knocked over by Calvin, who manages to keep them both balanced by holding on to her. He gazes at her in complete horror.

"Calvin! What are you doin' here?"

"Oh my god! You've got to get the hell out of here now!"

He grabs her wrist and drags her along. As they are making their way to the side entrance, people look on with concern and point their fingers.

"Heyyy, just what the hell do ya think you're doin', Cal?"

Now all of a sudden, there's a loud boom! The spirit growls and yells, "Sooo you got my bitch!" Then out of nowhere, *bam! Bam!* Floyd sank two bullets into Calvin's back! He and Val went crashing through the glass door. Now there's complete pandemonium in the club. "You think you're just getting away without giving me my money?"

"*Nooo*...you dumbass idiot!" Then the spirit launches a fireball at Floyd's face. Totally enraged now, it screams as glass begins to shatter all over the place! The front and back doors mysteriously lock in place. Lights start to flicker and pop! Mayhem ensues throughout the entire club. Patrons waiting at the front entrance take off running, screaming, "Fire!"

Val pushes Calvin off her and slowly lifts herself up. Looking crazily at him, she whispers, "Wha-wha-what just happened?"

Calvin gazes up at her, barely able to speak, he whispers back, "Ben...Ben did this. He...he was tryin' to get you. Please...please listen to me. Go to my place...Go to my room and look under the bed and you'll see a briefcase. It's...it's full of money. Take it and live...a...better life..."

She watches as he takes his last breath. "Oh...oh my god! *Nooo!* Calvin, Calvin, no!" She reaches over and hugs his lifeless body, sobbing. Suddenly, someone emerges from the smoke and flames completely engulfed, screaming! Startled out of her mind, Val jumps up and backs away from the flaming body coming toward her. It was Floyd. Putting a hand over her mouth, she screams. The body finally collapses and falls at her feet. Then surprisingly, another person comes out of the raging fire and immediately collapses to the pavement! It was...Paul?

Susan gets out of her car and instantly notices all the commotion. She takes off toward the club and then...*boom!* The explosion from the inside blew out the front entrance, sending a huge fireball with debris and black smoke billowing forth. She screams as she hits the ground. Club Boozy was now a raging inferno. Minutes later, sirens begin to sound from all directions. As Susan was regaining her composure, Val comes running up. She spreads her arms and Val collapses into her, crying. "Oh my god...what happened? Are you okay?"

Val just shivered and sobbed, not able to say a single word. She thought to herself, *Who the hell would even believe me?*

Hours later, after the firefighters finally put out the blaze, Val's in the hospital with Ranetta by her side. She got stitches from the deep cuts received going through the glass door. "It's over, Netta! It's all over!"

Ranetta gazes at her, crying and says, "What are you talkin' 'bout, Val? It's all over?"

"Apparently nobody's told you...The club, it's gone! It's gone up in flames!"

"What? What the hell...no, no, no...I haven't heard that! I need to call Floyd." She reaches for her phone as Val replies, "I'm sorry to tell you, Netta, but...he's gone too." She breaks down as Ranetta sits there with a blank stare and drops her phone to the floor.

After checking out, Val and Ranetta catch a ride with Susan. She heads to the club's parking lot to pick up the rental car that was left behind. Luckily, Val's purse was strapped on her shoulder the whole time, so she still had the keys. The only thing lost was her phone, which is why she couldn't enlighten Ranetta about what transpired earlier. Susan is the first to break the silence. "Do you know what happened, exactly?"

"All I can tell you is I heard a couple of gunshots, then I went flyin' through a glass door. A huge fire erupted and then an explosion."

"Gunshots? Oh my god...who got shot?"

"Please, Netta. Calm down...It was Calvin."

"Calvin...he's gone, too? Jesus! I don't understand it! What was he doin' at the club anyway? He just buried his cousin. Who would want to shoot him? Why?"

"I can't say for sure, but I do know that's how he was killed. Someone was chasing him because he ran into me, and we took off for the side door. I looked back briefly and saw Floyd running toward us. I turned away, and that's when I heard the shots, then we went through the glass door."

Susan interjects, "So...so you're sayin' Floyd shot Calvin? Oh my god!" Ranetta gasps for air and holds back a scream.

Val quickly adds, "I don't know for sure. He's the only one I seen when I glanced back." Deep down though, she knew the whole truth. She did hear the bellowing screams of Ben's spirit. She also figured out the money Calvin told her about was Floyd's. It had to be the mysterious stash Ranetta told her about that was stolen from the club. She couldn't mention Ben's involvement in front of Susan. She wouldn't understand. Besides, trying to explain it all would be a pure headache.

Eventually, they pull up to the ghastly sight. The building, which was still smoldering, was covered with black soot. Yellow caution tape was surrounding it now. A fire truck remained as a standby, and a few police cruisers continued to patrol the area. The trio approaches an officer who was chatting with the firemen.

"Excuse me, would it be alright if I picked up my rental car over there?" Val points in the direction of the car.

"Yes, by all means. We're trying to completely clear the whole area anyway."

Val looks over at Ranetta and says, "Okay, you ready?"

"Oh yeah...umm...Susan, thanks for everything. Please give me a call tomorrow. We can do lunch. We'll talk some more. There's a lot to unpack."

"No problem, none at all, considering the fact that we all have to look for other jobs...Oh my god! You two please, *please* be safe goin' home. Call me as soon as you get there."

Val says, "We will for sure. Thanks, girl!" She reaches over and gives her a big hug.

Susan whispers, "No problem, girl. I'll see you two tomorrow."

The two walk toward the car as Susan goes back to hers. Ranetta suddenly has a chill go over her body as she glanced over at the burned-down building. She stared at it one last time as the eeriness built, but soon dissipated when they pulled out of the parking lot and disappeared down the street.

As they're rolling along, Ranetta asks, "So it was definitely Floyd who shot Calvin, hun?"

"Yeah, unfortunately. He's also the one that stole Floyd's money."

"What? How do you know that?"

"Because before he died, he told me where he hid it and that he wanted me to have it."

"Oh my god...Seriously?"

"Yep, so exactly how much did Floyd say was stolen?"

"Sixty thousand."

Val's mouth dropped, and eyes widened as she blurts, "Sixty g's? Damn! He had that much hidden? I don't mean any disrespect, but if someone stole that from me, I'd shoot them too! Money like that is too hard to come by in this day and age!"

"Huh…in any day and age…So what about the explosion? Do you know what caused that?"

Val hesitates, then takes a long breath before she starts to explain. "Umm…Netta, I didn't want to say anything in front of Susan because she would've never understood it. You see, that catastrophe that happened back in Missouri has seemed to have followed us here."

Ranetta gazes over at her with a petrified look on her face and asks, "Ben?"

Now in a low voice she says, "Yep, I'm afraid so."

Ranetta starts to tear up, "Why? How? How did you know it was him?"

"Because I heard him clearly."

"Well…God was with you. You're still here…Oh gosh! You're still here! He missed you again!" There's nothing but silence, except for a few sniffles here and there, the rest of the way home.

The next afternoon, there's a knock on their door. Ranetta goes to answer, and it's Detective Lockett. He smiles as he asks, "You wouldn't happen to be Valencia Tucket?" He flashes his badge as she smiles back.

"No, who's asking?"

"I'm Detective Lamar Lockett. I talked to Ms. Tucket last night. I was given this address. Umm…does she live here?"

"Yes, she does. She's my niece. My name is Ranetta Gibbs. Please come on in." She steps aside as the detective walks by her.

"Thank you."

"Hey, Val, you got company!" She appears from the back looking confused. He extends his hand and introduces himself. Then she quickly says, "Oh yeah, now I remember…Huh, you know things went completely down the drain after I got off the phone with you."

"What the hell happened?"

"Welp, the only thing I can tell you is Calvin, one of my coworkers—"

"Wait...Calvin Kitchen? Oh yeah, that's right. He did work there! I guess I'ma have to talk to him as well. So as you were sayin'." She hangs her head and exhales loudly, then starts to explain again, "As I was sayin', we ended up crashing through a glass door at the side entrance, which is the reason I have all these stitches. He was being chased by the owner, Floyd, who ended up shooting him in the back. He died shortly after...unfortunately. I had to sit there and witness that."

"What? Are you kidding me? He's dead?"

"No! I'm not kidding you! What the cause of it all, I don't have a clue." Even though she did, she chose to keep her mouth shut about the money. "Do you know what caused the fire?"

"No." Once again knowing the truth, but could not say a word. The detective went on with the questioning and soon bid farewell and left. He was completely baffled about the whole situation; everything was still pretty much a mystery to him.

As the week went on, more details about the case leaked little by little. There's only a handful of bodies that could be identified. The rest were burned way beyond recognition. Rudolph yet again is plagued with arranging another funeral. It's set for Saturday at the same church where Rodney's funeral was held. Calvin will be laid to rest right next to his cousin.

It's Thursday, and Ranetta already has an interview for a management position at Sound Trust Bank. Val's at Greenbriar Mall applying for a retail job. Fortunately for the two, they land the jobs! Riding on the bus back home, though, Val thought about the stash of loot Calvin told her about. "Geesh...I'm glad I got this job, but we could still use that money! Boy, I hope no one's found it yet." Later, both decided to celebrate landing their new gigs by ordering Chinese food. They just wanted to stay in and count their blessings. They knew things could've been a lot worse—a whole lot worse! As they chow down on wonton soup and shrimp fried rice, Val asks, "How should I get the money, Netta? I know I can't just walk out the house with the briefcase in my hand, especially without being questioned."

"You're still thinking about getting that money? Someone's probably found it by now. I mean, with the funeral coming up and all."

"True...but what if they didn't? I'm still gonna try. Besides, he said I could have the money. It came straight from the horse's mouth."

"Yes, Val, that may be true, but it wasn't his to begin with. It was Floyd's."

Val smacks her lips and snaps, "Yeah...Floyd's no longer here either...I mean...no disrespect! We could really use that loot right now, Netta...maybe start our own business or whatever."

Ranetta sighs and falls silent for a moment, then says, "Maybe... it just all seems so crazy to me. It's so ironic if you think about it. Money was the direct root of evil in Missouri, as it's become here as well! I don't know, Val. It could be a bad omen."

"Yes, maybe, but I think the madness is over with. You know what...I have a big Coach bag that'll do the trick. I'll just go in with it empty, dump the money in it, put the briefcase back, and nobody will know. Yeah, that's what I'll do."

Saturday rolls around, Val and Ranetta attend Calvin's funeral. They're moved by the service more than they thought possible. The tears flowed honestly, and just as expected, they're invited back to the house for dinner. As the family was chatting and reminiscing, Val excused herself to go to the bathroom. She's able to sneak into Calvin's old room, closing the door behind her. Val rushes over to the bed, then peeks under and, sure enough, there's the briefcase! Quickly glancing back at the door to see if the coast was still clear first, she then reaches in and snatches it out to her.

Meanwhile, how nosy Nancy ended up at the house is anybody's guess because she wasn't actually invited. Yet she managed to show up anyway. She was there and up to her old tricks. She breaks away from the ongoing conversations in the living room and sneaks down the hallway. She approaches and opens one door; it's the laundry room. Immediately closing it, she moves on down the hall. Just before she grabs the doorknob to Calvin's old room, one of the family members starts to come down the hall. "Hey, you lookin' for something?"

Embarrassed and with a nervous voice, she says to Rudolph, "Heyyy…umm…kinda got turned around. Where's your bathroom?"

"Oh…it's the door on your right, but I think someone's in there already."

"Oh…okay…well, I guess I'll try it later, thanks."

"No problem," then he disappears into the laundry room. Nancy hurries down the hall and rejoins the others.

Not realizing she just dodged a bullet, courtesy of Rudolph, Val opens the case and beams at the neat stacks of money. She quickly dumps it all into her bulky Coach bag and slides the briefcase back under the bed. With the bag securely by her side, Val rushes to the door, opens it softly, and peeks out. Rudolph walks out of the laundry room, closing the door behind him, and proceeds down the hallway toward the living room. When he finally disappears around the corner, she slips out, shuts the door behind her, and quickly walks down the hallway.

Later on that evening, after returning home, Val strolls into Ranetta's room to show her the stash. "Welp, Netta, here it is!" She dumps the money on her bed.

With a shocked look on her face, Ranetta just stares at the rubber-banded stacks of cold hard cash! Finally, she says, "Oh my god! I haven't seen this much at one time in a long time! Sixty thousand dollars…wow!"

"Well…I don't know for sure. I haven't counted it yet."

"Well then, hey…let's get to it." They immediately begin to unwrap the bundles and count it. Shortly, they conclude that it's exactly sixty thousand to the tee!

Val asks, "Okay…so now what do we do?"

Ranetta thinks for a moment, "We need to put it in a safe place until we figure out what to do with it exactly."

"Hell…do you want to buy a safe?"

"Oh, no…I think that's too risky havin' that much cash around here. I was thinking about a safe deposit box at the bank I'm about to work for. I'll be able to keep a close eye on it, and by not having it in an account, we'll avoid any tax issues that could come up."

"Yeah, you right…we certainly don't need that."

"Besides, the damn measly interest they pay on a savings account sucks! There's no real money there."

Val snickers and says, "Will it all fit into a safe deposit box?"

"Actually, let's get two. You get one, and I'll get one. We can split the full amount in half; then it should all fit." Nodding her head in agreement, Val then smiles and says, "Okay, cool, let's do that!"

Across town, Nancy meets up with Rudy. "Man...I just can't believe what has happened, Nancy! My cousin's gone, the damn club is gone! How? Why?"

"All I know, Rudy, is that there was a lot of strange shit goin' on around there! Floyd babblin' wit' a evil spirit and all! And it be talkin' back to him, too!"

"Whoa, whoa, whoa! What the hell are you talkin' 'bout, Nancy? A spirit? Where did dat come from?"

"Well, actually...some of what I'm sayin' stems from this." She slides something across the table to him. He picks up the journal, then thumbs through it a bit and eventually looks up at her, bewildered and frowning. "So what the hell is this?"

"Hey, it's something I found in the men's restroom trash can a week before you performed at the club. Your boy Calvin came stormin' out the restroom when I was about to go in and finish cleaning. No one else was in there, even though I know I heard him yellin' at somebody. I know he left it behind for sure because I'd already emptied out the trash bins and put new bags in them. I also found these." She reaches into her purse to pull out some small candles, then puts them on the table.

Rudy shrugs, "Okay...so what the hell does all this supposed to mean, exactly? What, you think Calvin had something to do with all this mess that's happened?"

"Him and Floyd were arguing that night before the place went up in flames. Them along wit' dat evil spirit! Floyd wanted to know where his money was. The spirit was blaming Calvin, and he was blamin' the spirit. Then it started to order Calvin to tell Floyd about the deal they made. It was somethin' 'bout dat chick, Val. Then he started screamin' 'bout how he wanted her soul. Calvin will get the money, and he would bring her to the spirit! Then he mentioned somethin' even stranger. It was that the original deal was made back in KC after some club burned down to the ground, courtesy of him."

Rudy's eyes bulged as he stared blankly into space. He thinks back to that night his cousin and Ranetta were talking about the club she used to manage that had burned down. The very same one he performed in that night and by the grace of God, left just before the horrid affair. "I heard there were gun shots fired! Umm…do you know who got shot?"

"Yeah, before I got outta there, I saw Floyd shoot Calvin in the back."

"What the! Damnnn! So he got 'im?"

"Yep, he got 'im, and well…"

Rudy's curious about the slight pause. He immediately asks, "Well, what?"

"Well…what about the money? It's still out there somewhere. I figure if we find it, we can split it."

He laughs. "We? Huh…why should I share my cousin's money with you?"

She bluntly states, "Cuz I'm the one bringin' you this valuable information, fool! I totally deserve a cut! I didn't have to tell you shit! You got it?"

Smirking now, he replies, "Okay! Okay! I was just bullshittin' ya! You do deserve a cut, no doubt."

Rolling her eyes, she quips, "Umm, hmm…you damn right!"

On the evening news, the authorities finally release some of the names of the victims that were unidentifiable after the club blaze. "Paul Ward, age 27, Floyd Clinton, age 45, and Latrell Duncan, age 24, were all taken by the fire. Calvin Kitchen was confirmed to be shot in the back twice and died just outside the club, according to the coroner's report. Ward and Duncan, along with two other unidentified men who were taken by the blaze, are suspects in a current rape case concerning a twenty-three-year-old woman, whose name has been withheld. Duncan and an accomplice, Derrick Sampson, who also perished in the fire, are the ones responsible for Rodney Clemens's death a few weeks ago. Floyd Clinton was the owner of the popular night spot, Club Boozy's, and Calvin Kitchen was an employee at the club. There's been no word as to why he was shot nor who the assailant was. Reporting live from this tragic site, Chad Knoxville for Action News Seven."

"Thanks, Chad, we just got word in that the death toll from this tragedy is 106. Such a sad time in Atlanta right now. Our hearts and prayers go out to all the families who've lost their loved ones."

Impacted by what the anchorwoman just stated, Ranetta shakes her head in deep sadness and says, "Oh my lord…it's such a shame! Pure evilness! That's all there is to it! Pure evilness! It'll never be known about how it all really went down! Those poor innocent souls who perished so unnecessarily, and God forgive me, the only good things that came from all this madness is you're still alive, and you don't ever have to worry about those thugs who assaulted you again!"

Val, in a low voice, says, "Yeah, I guess you're right, Netta."

But later on that evening, as she was lying in bed, she's stumbling over the last statement her aunt made as they were watching the news. She's very thankful to be alive, and the fact that Calvin redeemed himself at the end was a plus! She also couldn't help but relish in the fact that those assholes got what they deserved and, ironically, at the hands of her father! Val now smiles and soon drifts off to sleep, but what she didn't realize was she had Floyd to thank for giving those goons free passes to the club in the first place. Secondly, the irony continues, something she absolutely has no clue of, and it's the money! It was actually her father's to begin with! Yep, Val went on to dreaming, totally unaware of the unsuspecting revenge.

The End

About the Author

Edward C. Knox was born in 1970, in Des Moines, Iowa. Growing up in Atlanta, Georgia, though, he found his artistic talent at an early age. Drawing has always been a big part of his life, but he later discovered a passion for writing in 2008. It's been a long road, but the journey into the world of writing has begun.

Putting together the book was challenging, but a fun process for the most part. Mystery, sci-fi, and the supernatural have always been points of interest. Growing up watching these genres play out became the sole inspiration for writing this novel.

Printed in the USA
CPSIA information can be obtained
at www.ICGtesting.com
LVHW090928270924
792207LV00002B/299